BORN

TO

LUST

BORN TO LUST

JOHNNY ARCHER

J. Archer Publications
Palm Bay, Florida

Acknowledgment

This book is dedicated to all the women who in some way touched my life, especially my mother, who defied the odds by raising six wonderful children by herself. The experiences I had with all of you have molded me into the man I am today.

Whether positive or negative, I have learned much about life and myself. From time to time I think of each of you and wonder where you are and how you are doing. I must admit that most of you were very sophisticated and decent ladies, deserving much better than you received from me. For that I'd like to apologize for any hurt or suffering I may have caused. Don't think that I got off scot-free. We all have to pay. You reap what you sow, and I paid dearly. My biggest battle was with myself. As I searched the wickedness of my soul to deal with the demons of my past I gained understanding and found comfort in the book of Proverbs.

Also, I'd like to give special thanks to the mothers of my children. Each of you is extra special in your own way, and unique to the world. I pray, more for some than others, that we can maintain a cordial relationship for the sake of our children. After all, they are ours for life.

Here's a 5-star thanks to Kareen, my better half and the mother of my youngest child, for being humble enough to put up with me. I thank you for all your understanding and for your effort in the editing of this book.

Further, I dedicate this book in memory of my good friend James (Jimmy Jet) Roberts who died from liver cancer at the young age of 27. You will always be with me...thanks for the memories.

Sexual Beginning

I began to learn about my sexuality at the age of six, while in the first grade. In the classroom we sat at round tables in groups consisting of boys and girls. Every day I sat next to the same little girl and whenever the teacher wasn't looking, I would put my hand inside her panties and play with her stuff every chance I got. I really didn't know what it was supposed to smell like because each time I finished playing with her and smelled my hand, it would smell like shit. No wonder she was always laughing. Maybe she was fully aware her ass was stinking.

I can say that I had the time of my life in first grade playing between the legs of a skinny first grader. This would explain why I had difficulty with my reading. I was spending too much time finger fucking and not enough time with phonics. By the time I entered second grade I wasn't too good at reading but I was real good at keeping my hand in the drawers of the girl next to me. I recall talking to one of the girls in my class named Risa. Our teacher, Mrs. Brown, put both of us in the closet. The closet door pulled down like a garage door, closing completely. For the next hour I fondled Risa in every way imaginable and even tried to put my thing in hers. She was laughing and making noise so Mrs. Brown made us leave the closet, ending my fun. Every day I tried to get in trouble with Risa so Mrs. Brown would put us in the closet—but she never did it again. I often wonder if she smelled Risa's stuff on my hand.

CHAPTER 1

NEW BEGINNING

Life started for me in the year 1950. I lived in a wooden shack on Erving Avenue in St. Petersburg, Florida with my mother, four sisters, and a brother. The house was set up high on blocks, had a shingled roof, five windows, and three wooden steps that led to the front porch and creaked each time you walked on them. There were two bedrooms, a living room, dining room, and a kitchen. The only bathroom in the house had a toilet and a sink; the steel washtub used for bathing was situated in the middle of the kitchen.

Times were hard for my mother mainly because she had six children—of whom I was the youngest—and no husband. She worked six days a week doing all sorts of odd jobs to support us. Having a family of my own and knowing how difficult it is to raise children, I can imagine how difficult it must have been for her. But I've come to learn that single, oppressed women with children go through and endure things that ordinary mothers would never experience.

My mother moved to St. Petersburg in 1947 to join her husband, who had relocated there due to problems with white folks in Georgia. Seeking refuge, they moved in with his aunt. The trouble he ran from in Georgia eventually followed him to St. Petersburg, so he disappeared late one night, leaving her and five children behind. That night was the last time she enjoyed the pleasure or the comfort of her husband. He was nowhere to be found and she didn't hear from him for a long time.

Having no one to turn to for help she remained with her husband's aunt. Aunt Mammie was old and scary looking with snowy-white, stringy hair. She was tall and thin in stature with large feet and hands that complemented her appearance. She lacked compassion, since she knew she was the only relative living in the city, and took advantage of my mother. Aunt Mammie treated her badly, taking virtually all of the money my mother earned for rent after six days of tedious work, leaving her with very little for anything else. Not in a position to retaliate, my mother endured the terrible treatment until she could do better.

One day my mother was talking to a neighbor who was aware of the mistreatment she was enduring. The good neighbor offered to baby-sit for free while my mom worked. Being the kindhearted neighbor that she was, she gave my mother the down payment for the apartment on Erving Avenue. My mother was an expert at surviving. Survival was something I learned from her early in life, and like her, I became a master at it.

My mother was 5'6" with a medium build and a shapely body. She had a beautiful pecan-brown complexion, shoulder-length hair, and sparkling eyes that accentuated her oblong face. She was a knock-out at twenty-two. My father was about 5'7" with a pot belly. He was ruggedly handsome with curly black hair to match his dark skin complexion. My dad and mom met while living in Georgia during my mom's previous marriage. Dad had come to her house to purchase moonshine from her husband. For Dad, meeting her again after she was husbandless was a gift from God. For her it also was a blessing. She had five children and he wanted her, he had none and she needed him. Of course, if the truth be told he had to be a damn idiot to fall in love with a woman with five children. What the hell was he thinking? But I must give them credit, he wanted her, she needed the help, and my black ass wanted to be born.

My mom always gave my dad credit for helping her through the most difficult times. He continued to help until I was about five years old, then he completely disappeared from my life and hers. I guess the weight from all of the responsibilities of maintaining a family, as well as the difficulties of being a black man during his time finally took its toll. I resented him leaving, and felt rejected and unloved. About two years after he stopped showing up, I received a package from Cincinnati, Ohio, containing several shirts with an alligator logo design on the pocket. That was the last gift I would receive from him. I guess the only other good thing he did for me was to give me the nickname Pookey, which would later become synonymous with good-looking women.

My next door neighbor was an old lady named Margerie who had features like those of a gypsy. She was also my godmother, and a good one she was. With my mother working all the time, my godmother became totally responsible for my care. She was crazy about me and gave me a lot of love and attention, even more than my mother did at times. But this I'm sure was due to the amount of hours my mom worked. I remember that Margerie grew sugar cane and always made sure that I ate my share. My family stayed next door to her until I was three years old, then we moved up in status to the east side of Erving Avenue to the projects, better known as Jordan Park.

I learned so much from my godmother. Like my mother, she had mastered the technique of surviving. An entrepreneur of her time, she sold moonshine to the men in the hood; anything to make a dollar. I still got to see her quite often after we moved since she was the only babysitter I would allow to take care of me. My godmother continued to look after me in every way until her death in 1959. I credit her for my gift of gab, she had plenty.

Even though I didn't know it at the time, I was the most creative of my siblings, the most adventurous and the most unruly. Ironically, I was afraid of ghost, but that was only fitting for the devil himself.

I remember some of the things that went on in my neighborhood. Affairs that included my dad, and his womanizing, which probably set the stage for the dog I would become. I remember one Sunday morning—one of those rare times I spent with him—he took me to a lady's house where drinking among other things took place. He told me to remain in the car until he got back. Unknown to him, I sneaked out to take a peek and saw him hugging and kissing a woman. As soon as I reached home I told my mother everything I had seen. Well, because of my tattling, I was banned from ever going out with him again. As a matter of fact, until I reached the age of twelve I never saw my dad but once or twice after that event.

Moving to Jordan Park was definitely a step up for us. We went from a two-bedroom shack to a three-bedroom apartment, with heat I might add. Of course, there was no air conditioning; but, you don't miss what you never had. We had each other, and that's all that mattered. The apartment was two stories with all of the bedrooms and the one bathroom sited on the upper floor. The first floor had a big living room with an eat-in kitchen toward the rear.

The housing project was very beautiful with a combination of one- and two-story buildings running parallel and perpendicular to each other along with sidewalks all around. Our apartment was parallel to the alley that ran the full length of the project. To the left was a thick layer of palmetto palms about 15-feet tall. Each unit had its own private yard with a huge royal palm at the edge of the yard. Directly in front of our building was a large, open green field with massive oak trees planted in each of the four corners, making the scenery more beautiful. Life was good for all of us compared to whence my mother had come.

The project was full of life and had lots of children of all ages. We played all kinds of games—football, basketball, baseball, and some others that we invented. Sometimes we played hopscotch, jump rope, and marbles with the girls. We even had our own movie theater, just for coloreds. What a life!

CHAPTER 2

GROWING UP

In the fall of 1954, I started kindergarten at MacAdams Day School. My brother walked with me to school the first day, took me to the classroom and when I realized that he was leaving me I cried and cried. He didn't seem to care about my troubles, so my teacher Mrs. Caster came over, hugged me and told me everything would be all right. She asked me if I wanted to go outside and play and I said yes, getting happier by the minute. When we got to the playground she introduced me to her son, Poppe, a tiny kid much smaller than me.

I remember he was playing with a little red wagon. I stood and watched for a while, not knowing what to play with, and then observed a larger kid who had taken over the wagon and had Poppe pushing him. I ran over to them, pushed the big kid out of the wagon and he landed on his head. He started crying. From that day on Poppe became my best friend at school and no one bothered him after that. I had a lot of fun in kindergarten and everyday seemed to be a better one. For the next two years, I had Poppe and the bully push me in the wagon during free play.

Shortly after moving to Jordan Park I met Robbie who later became my best friend. He and his two sisters lived with their dad. Their mother had died several years earlier. I liked his dad because he spent a lot of time with me. He was the only male role model in my life and he treated me the same way he treated little Robbie. Wherever he took his son, he took me, even if my mother didn't have the money for me to go. Robbie's youngest sister, Muffin, and I were six years old and in the same class. I liked her because she would always allow me to touch and feel on her booty. When we would go out to free play none of the other boys liked doing square dancing. But I liked it because I could hold Muffin and feel on her when the teacher wasn't looking. I always seemed to have good instincts on how to maneuver myself into position with girls.

One day during summer vacation I was showing off to try to impress Muffin. Robbie was mopping the concrete floor of the porch using a lot of soap. He was imitating James Brown by singing, dancing, and moving his feet as if he was the real thing. He was two years older than me and couldn't care less about girls. Little sporty me was jumping high out of a chair, yelling, "Superman!" and then sliding as if I had just landed after leaping from a tall building. Muffin was peeping out of the door with a big smile, enjoying the entertainment. Noticing her interest, I repeated my performance. This time I landed on my heels, sliding as my feet kicked up in the air and I came down on the back of my head. Blood was streaming out everywhere. I had burst a hole in my head the size of a tennis ball. I heard Robbie scream, "Oh my God!"

I got up in excruciating pain and started running home. By now blood had completely covered my shirt and part of my pants. My friend was running behind me telling me not to run. To this day I still don't know why he was telling me not to run. I was the one with the tennis-ball size hole in my head, and bleeding to death, so what else was I to do but run for help? The news of me bursting my head and my inevitable death spread like wildfire. It's a good thing that my life wasn't determined by the critics because I wouldn't be writing this book.

By the time I got halfway home everyone in the neighborhood was running behind me. As I pushed the back door of my house open, I screamed to my mother to help me because I was dying. She wrapped my head in a bunch of towels and rushed me to the hospital. They shaved all the hair off my head and put in about 100 stitches to close the large hole. I remained in the hospital for about one week and was restricted from playing for a couple of months until my wound had completely healed. All my friends came to see me, and Muffin said she cried because she wanted me to be all right. Now you know that made me feel better. From that day on I never played Superman again nor have I watched it on television.

During my elementary years, I blossomed to be one of the top athletes in the school. I was a member of the YMCA, participating in all sports available. We had an archery team but only two of us showed up to participate. At the end of the season we had a contest between the different elementary schools. My teammate didn't show up so I had to compete alone against all of the other schools. Proud to say, I won the trophy by scoring more points than any member from the other teams.

I played basketball on the school intramural team and we made it to the finals. For the first time ever, the two finalist teams were allowed to play in the college gymnasium, before the college basketball team participated. My team dominated the tournament, walking away with the trophy. Once again, my light shone bright. I remember graduation day when I received the top medals in every category— basketball, archery, swimming, and gymnastics—except one, where I finished second.

Junior high school started out as I had anticipated— lots of beautiful girls. It was lunchtime when I spotted the finest and most stunning girl in the entire school. She was tall for an eighth grader and had a chocolate complexion, almond-shaped eyes, neatly braided hair, and a smile that would brighten up any room. Her breasts were full and overlooked her small waist and full hips. Her body was cut so graciously, as if carved by a sculptor. She was so sweet, everyone called her Caramel. And sugar she was, bubbling brown sugar with a honey glaze. Every part of me focused on her and nothing but her. I started to inquire as to whether or not she had a boyfriend but received very little information since she didn't live in the project. My friend Manny and I talked about her constantly over the next few days until I saw her again in the lunchroom. Confident and cool as I was, I approached her and started to go through my scoop ritual that I had developed.

"Excuse me," I said. "My name is Johnny, may I ask yours?"

"Caramel," was her response.

"You are very pretty."

"Thank you," she said, flaunting her beautiful smile and pearly-white teeth.

"God must have been real happy when he made you," I said, hoping to make an impression. She smiled. "Where do you live?" I asked.

"On the North Side."

"Are you seeing anyone?"

"Not really. But I'm interested in one of your friends."

"Which one of my friends?" I asked, trying not to show my disappointment.

"Manny."

Acting cool, I said, "I guess this is not my lucky day."

"I wouldn't say that...he may not like me."

Still trying to impress her, I said, "If he doesn't, something is definitely wrong with his brain. Well, if I can't have you for myself, maybe we can be friends."

"I'd like that," she said as she turned to leave.

My friend Manny was a little slow with girls so I figured I still had a chance. Her being interested in him didn't agitate me because my loyalty was to me, especially when it came to a girl I wanted. It was every man for himself.

Typically, I was a very impatient individual, but I learned early in life that patience was indeed a virtue. Believe me, I was like a lion lying in the tall grass waiting for the right opportunity to capture its prey and if I had to wait a lifetime, I was determined to get her in my bed.

As time went on, Caramel and Manny started going together so I watched and waited, letting her know how much I cared for her every chance that I got.

The following summer she moved into the project a couple of row houses behind me. I took that as a blessing and felt that it would surely improve my chances.

One day Caramel, Swet, (one of my neighborhood friends and classmates) and I were at Manny's house alone. Caramel wanted some attention so she went upstairs waiting for Manny to show up. He looked at me and said he didn't know what to do. I told him to stay downstairs and I'd go and warm her up for him. When I got upstairs, she was lying on the bed. I told her that Manny was a little nervous and that I would keep her company for a while until he gained his confidence. I started touching her softly then kissed her on the arms and neck.

Getting no rejection, I started kissing her on the mouth, slowly inserting my tongue through her now parted lips. I knew she was in heat by her body movements so I put my hands into her panties to intensify her some more. By this time, about ten minutes had passed when Manny came upstairs with an attitude after he saw what I was doing. I told him that I was only warming her up for him. I returned downstairs with one hard-ass dick. And damn was I pissed. Well, Caramel got frustrated for some reason and left— nobody got any pussy that day. But I kept the faith, busying myself by chasing just about all the good-looking, fine girls inside and outside of the project.

About one week or so after the incident at Manny's house, he and Caramel broke up and I knew it was just a matter of time before I got to that thing. All Manny had to do that day in his house was do what he saw me doing and put that dick in the hole.

Caramel had every reason to leave his sorry ass. A limp dick can't keep a woman happy. A lady needs a man who will ram that dick in her every chance he gets. Put the fucking dick all up in her ass was all he had to do. I still laugh when I remember him telling me he didn't know what to do.

One night I went on the prowl and happened to stop by Caramel's house. I could see her through the screened door lying on the couch. I knocked on the door.

"Who is it?" she asked.

"It's me, Pookey."

"Come in," she replied.

"Hi, how are you?"

"I'm fine," she said.

"Yes, you are!" I said, playing with words and smiling mischievously. You are damn fine, I whispered to myself.

"Where is everyone?" I inquired as I surveyed the room. Positioning herself on the couch, she replied, "My mom is upstairs and everyone else is out...only God knows where."

"Can I sit down and keep you company for a while?"

"Sure."

"You are still the most beautiful girl in the world," I said, as I sat down beside her on the couch.

Smiling, she replied, "You always say that!"

"That's because it is true. I've loved you since the first day I saw you in the cafeteria," I said, while touching her gently on the arm. She showed no resistance as my whole body went into metamorphosis. I started trembling, my smile got brighter and my dick got harder than steel, juice running, letting me know it was pussy time. The room was dark, illuminated only by the television. She lay back on the couch that was to the left of the front door next to the staircase wall. The television was on the opposite side with a small coffee table in the middle of the room. I guess she remembered how good it had felt at Manny's house. I started by kissing her, feeling on one breast, while sucking the nipple of the other firm, young titty. I then inserted my hand in her panties and knew then that the pussy was all mines. Patience is a motherfucker but I had plenty when pussy was involved.

My moment of truth had finally arrived as I slowly removed her panties. I kissed her hard again and spread her legs. While sucking on her nipples I removed my dick from my pants, which were already unzipped. As I started to plant my seed the door swung wide open. It was her brother, who was older and bigger than me. I jumped up with my dick still hard and joy-juice dripping all over my pants, her legs, and the couch. I tried to put my dick back in my pants, but it was too long and too hard. With my rod extended far out in front of my fly I broke for the back door at top speed, praying every step of the way that it wasn't locked. I sprinted to the safety of my house trying hard not to trip over myself. From that day on, every time I walked by her house someone was watching me. There was no stopping me at that point because I knew in my heart that I was going to get it. My patience was stronger than ever.

CHAPTER 3

LOSS OF A FRIEND

The new hangout spot was Chunky's Corner, a teen club that had recently opened on the main drag. It was located at the southeast corner of the main intersection. The Harden grocery store was to the west, the funeral home to the north, and the ice-cream parlor was diagonally across in the northwest corner. The project was situated just behind the Harden store.

I would go to the teen club after school and on weekends to play pinball, pool, and cards. They served hamburgers, hot dogs, and of course, very good milkshakes. But my main reason for going was to check out the babes that showed up every day. On this particular Sunday my boy Boot and I were hanging out at the club, sitting at the counter having a milkshake while talking with two pretty young things. We were dressed down to the bone and looking good. We had planned our strategy, selected our victims earlier that day, and had our game on real good.

About an hour after we arrived at the joint someone came over to the counter and said, "Boot, your brother is outside fighting."

Both of us rushed out and sure enough it was his brother. Boot, a few others, and I broke up the fight. We then escorted his brother home and demanded that he stay there and not return to the teen club. Feeling good that we had done the right thing we headed back to the club to the two honeys that were waiting for us. We ordered another round of shakes and talked impressively in an attempt to score.

We were enjoying the girls' company and having fun when someone again came to the counter and said, "Boot, your brother is outside fighting." Once again, we ran outside and saw the brawl taking place in the middle of the street. Standing next to me, Boot reached down to stop the fight. In the midst of trying to break up the dispute, a loud bang from gunfire filled the air. I could tell that the shot came from behind me because I felt the sensation on my neck. Everyone fell to the ground fearing for their life. At that time I didn't know who had fired the gun or if anyone was hurt.

Moments later when we all felt that the danger had passed we got up from the ground. Everyone stood up except my friend Boot. He had been shot in the back and was unable to move. People were screaming, crying, and yelling for someone to call for an ambulance. Knowing how serious it was I ran as fast as I could to Boot's house, telling his parents the news of what had happened. Disarrayed, petrified and frightened with tears running down their faces, they gathered themselves and rushed to their son's side.

That day was the most painful and horrible time of my life. I don't think anyone in town who was aware of Boot being shot slept that night. When I got home my mother was in tears as she had already heard the news.

The next day during school everyone was very concerned as to Boot's condition. I was told earlier that day by his brother Manny that his condition hadn't changed.

Two days later at approximately noon, the announcement came over the loudspeaker that Boot had died. Darkness and silence covered our school and the heart of every black person in the city. Boot was one of the most likable and adorable kids in our community. He had become the most talked about basketball player of a long list of great talent. He was definitely the most likely to succeed. I won't write about his funeral because up to this day it is still a painful feeling.

I miss my friend. Although gone in flesh, his memory still lives in my heart. Almost forty years since Boot's death, his picture remains untouched on a table in his parents' home. Each time I visit them, I look closely at his picture and pray that he is in a better place.

CHAPTER 4

RUNNING FOR MY LIFE

September 1965 I was in high school, still chasing women. There was this little honey who was somewhat short, but had the biggest ass you have ever seen. Her name was Von and she lived with her aunt and a bunch of cousins, all female. I was after one of her cousins at first but she was playing hard-to-get, probably because she had her eyes on a friend of mine who also lived in the project. Realizing that I had little chance of scoring with my first choice I quickly diverted my attention to the cousin. After all, I only wanted to make a pit stop then move on. The good part about this situation was that the cousin liked me and that spelled instant sex without any hassle, the best kind.

During school one day I informed Von that I would be coming over to her house that night. She had already enlightened me as to the nights her aunt wouldn't be at home as she was a frequent dog track visitor. My mother also enjoyed going to the dog track and as long as she was winning she would stay and play. This I hoped would be the case with her aunt.

After school that day I went to my brother and got a French tickler, a condom with fingerlike projectiles. He had brought a collection of them back from Germany while in the army.

This time I didn't have to worry about unzipping my pants because this pussy was ripe and promised to me. I didn't have to work hard or run any games on this chick; my charisma had already got me over the hump. I arrived at her house just after dark as planned. The daylight hours were unsafe because with me chasing a lot of girls I could not afford to be seen. Knowing the expected time of my arrival, Von was waiting for me at the back door. She greeted me with soft kisses and tight hugs, held my hand and led me straight to her bedroom.

The house was rectangular with front and back porches and a long hallway dividing the house in half. Von's room was at the right front side of the house with one window that opened to the porch. Her room had a set of bunk beds; probably because there were so many of them in a house with limited space. The good thing was that Von had the lower bunk.

Since the bed was so small I decided to undress her before we got in. I'm sure her intention to make love was the same as mine because she wore very little. And when that little doesn't include drawers, the guessing is over. I undressed her first then myself. Upon the removal of my shirt she commented on my muscular chest as she sucked lightly on my nipples. After removing my pants and underwear while Von was still sucking on my nipples, she reached down and grabbed my big, hard cock. She put a second hand on it, looked me in the eyes and said, "It takes two hands to handle the Whopper."

Yeah, but only one tight pussy, I thought to myself as I started kissing her then slowly moved my mouth to the attention of her nipples. Lying on my side, I took my free hand and started rubbing on her thighs, purposely avoiding touching any part of her vagina.

After arousing her for a few minutes more I rubbed my finger lightly across her furry hairs, played with her clitoris then finger fucked her until sweat balls appeared all over her body. I put the French rubber on and eased into her wetness, listening as she let out a loud moan. For the next hour we fucked rhythmically as she came over and over again, clutching and holding me, begging me to cum. Because I loved fucking more than anything I know, I learned how not to cum too quickly. But she was concerned about her aunt's return so I increased my strokes and changed my rhythm, becoming mentally focused on the feeling in the head of my penis. Feeling the blood rush to the head, I had barely completed cumming when I heard the slamming of the screened door.

We were unaware that her aunt's car had pulled into the driveway since her cousins had not warned us. Unknown to me, each of them had boyfriends in their rooms. The only saving grace for them was that their rooms were located at the rear of the house, which gave them time to escape. Von's room was in the front next to the porch so I had no time to get dressed, much less leave. When her aunt entered through the screened door to the front porch I got under the bunk bed. There I was under the bed in an old dusty house, hot, stinking, and naked, and most of all trapped with nothing in my hand but my dick. I had heard around school that this lady was crazy and would shoot anyone caught around her daughters or niece. I was fucked, but I had patience.

I waited while she sat on the porch at the door's entrance of the shotgun house. The room I was in was a long way from the back door. I was fucked!

After a few minutes her aunt got up, walked in the house and said, "It smells like fish in here. Have someone been cooking in this house?"

"No, Mama, nobody been cooking in here," was the simultaneous response.

"All right," was her aunt's reply, "but it sure smells fishy to me."

At that point I was lying on my stomach with my face in my clothes trying to keep from sneezing, but worse than that I had to fart so I was squeezing my ass together trying to hold the gasses in. I was thinking, "God, if I can't hold it, I sure hope it's one of those quiet poots." I was in serious trouble 'cause it was coming. Out came a loud succession of farts. Von quickly said, "Excuse me," taking the blame. Fortunately for me, Mama thought that one of her daughters' boyfriends was in the house. She thought her niece was the sweetest little girl, and I was thinking, yeah Baby, sweet she is.

Mama decided to go back on the porch. Already half drunk of scotch, she started to doze. What a break that was for me. I eased my body from under the bed, grabbed my clothes, unintentionally left one shoe and ran down the shotgun hallway faster than a black man running from the KKK—the French tickler was still on my swinging dick, banging against my nuts. Halfway down the hall Mama awoke, looked up and saw me naked as the day I was born. She pointed her .38 revolver, which was already in her lap, and cut loose several rounds striking the wall on the right side and above my head. By that time I was hurdling the railing on the back porch, which was about eight feet above the ground. I ran the whole way home—roughly one mile. I was so scared I never once thought about whether or not I was shot.

When I got home I ran through the back door of my house stark naked, the rubber tickler still on my dick, trembling like a leaf on a tree. My mom was in the kitchen. She looked at me, knew what I had been doing and fell back into her chair and burst out laughing as if she was crazy.

She paused for a second and said, "Get a bath and take your black ass to bed."

That was the first and last time I got that pussy.

CHAPTER 5

HAVING FUN CHASING THE HONEYS

My boy Hawkbeek and I were hanging out together chasing them honeys one day. Hawkbeek stood at 5'7" with a muscular frame, fair skin, curly hair, and a teasing smile. He received his nickname because his nose curled down like the beak of a hawk. We had known each other since elementary school and were friends from the first day we met. We had a lot of things in common and our personalities were somewhat similar. Naturally, we partook in many activities together, especially sports. We were on the football team, and like me, he was very talented. Hawkbeek, however, was restricted from doing a lot of things as he had the responsibility of babysitting his little sister. Also, his mother was one strict person and would kick his ass at the drop of a hat if he violated any of her rules.

Hawkbeek and I were talking to two female friends named Beth and Gila. We were trying to arrange a time and place where all four of us could get together. This was difficult to do since we were in school during the week and one, if not both of our parents were home on the weekend. So the next thing to do was play hooky from school when no one was around. We arranged to meet the following Tuesday at a predetermined location close to Hawkbeek's house, since that was to be the love nest. My house was not a good place to meet because I had very nosey neighbors who stayed home all day—informing on me would be their greatest thrill.

The night before the big day we checked with the girls, ensuring that everything was in place.

Tuesday morning my parents and Hawkbeek's had left for work. I was thinking, what a sophisticated plan I came up with. Well, my boy and I left home as usual like we were on our way to school, but then detoured to rendezvous with our little love birds. We were just outside the project on one of the main streets when we saw a city bus go by, two blocks away from where the girls were supposed to meet us. Hawkbeek went into hysteria, screaming and shouting that the bus was the one his mother took and she saw him. I was trying to calm him down by telling him that his mother caught the 6:30 a.m. bus, and there was no way she could have seen him because he was still asleep when she was leaving to catch the bus. Then he started saying that if his mother wasn't on the bus, one of her friends was, and they saw him. By that time I was mad as hell because I had pussy two blocks away, no place to take Gila, who was my girl, and no money.

"Fuck the bus and whoever was on it. I've got pussy on my mind!" I shouted. "If someone saw me and told my mother, I'd make up an excuse, and if that didn't work I know that fucking Gila would be well worth the ass whooping I'd get, and right now I'll take the beating for some pussy," I continued.

"I'm scared and I can't take anymore of my mama's whoopings," Hawkbeek said looking at me frightfully.

"What are we going to do?" I asked.

His reply was one I did not want to hear. "I don't know what you are going to do, but I'm taking my ass to school right now."

He turned, faced the direction of the school and took off running faster than a speeding bullet, leaving me baffled. I knew his mother would kick his ass, but damn, not like that.

Well, I did the only thing left for me to do and that was to go to the site where the girls were waiting. When I got to the location, no one was there. The girls didn't show up. What a fucking bummer. I was standing there wondering if maybe Hawkbeek knew something and didn't tell me, because if he did, I was going to kick his ass. I quickly dismissed the thought because there was no way he would risk getting killed just to jive me. Something had gone wrong that day and I would find out, but whatever the case, I would prevail victoriously. So, off to school I went. Late, but I didn't give a damn.

Good friends never stay angry at each other for very long, especially if they have fun together. My motto was, "Never let a bad situation interfere with progress."

Hawkbeek told me about his new girlfriend Ann, and that she had a sister named Thia. He had already talked to Ann about setting me up with Thia, who agreed that I could come over and visit. We chose a time when their mother would be away from the house.

The date was set for Saturday morning about mid-day, allowing time for the girls to complete their chores. When we arrived at the house Hawkbeek and Ann went directly upstairs to the bedroom at the front of the house. He told me that I could use the bedroom on the back, which was the mother's room. Knowing him, I should have recognized some shit was up because nobody gives up the opportunity to have sex in a girl's mama's bed. As my focus was not on anything except convincing this young lady that making love to me was the right thing to do, I didn't bother to confront him. The one thing I had in my favor was that Thia knew that her sister was upstairs making love. Hawkbeek had already been intimate with Ann so he got busy right away. But being my first time with Thia I had to run my game down, in other words, beg if that's what it took. Begging didn't bother me because I felt it was all right to beg as long as I got the prize. After about fifteen minutes Thia agreed for us to go upstairs.

I started in on her with my usual technique, placing soft teasing kisses on her mouth then on the sensitive spots around her neck and ears while at the same time fondling her breasts with my hands. I would detour with my tongue to lick her nipples, alternating with light sucking. As always, I focused on the eyes because they would let me know her mood and reveal her weakness. I noticed that they were getting glossy and rolling back, disappearing behind her eyelids, so I moved my hand down inside her panties.

While feeling the wetness of her excitement I noticed her eyes were completely closing. She moaned and moved her body as if I had already entered her. Teasing her to a state of sexual agony, but not enough to make her cum, I eased my hard cock in her already saturated canal, fucking her as she screamed aloud passionately, begging me not to stop. Her movement increased, and the vital signs of her body gave testimony to the explosion building within her. She was about to cum. I skillfully increased my strokes, being careful not to upset her state of ecstasy, while matching and maintaining her rhythm pattern. I felt myself cumming with her as we clutched each other tightly, allowing our cum to unite us. Afterwards, I could see that she was drained; but the expression on her face and in her eyes painted a picture of true satisfaction never before experienced.

Relaxing with her still lying beneath me, we were complimenting each other when we were suddenly interrupted by footsteps running down the stairs and Hawkbeek shouting loudly. I didn't hear him clearly, as I was still focused on the legs wrapped around my waist.

He shouted again from downstairs, "Pookey, her mother is coming in the front door!"

Having started his little fuck session before I did, he had sufficient time to relax as well as get dressed. Hawkbeek wasn't being so generous after all. He knew all the time that the front bedroom would afford him the opportunity to see the mother's return, therefore, enabling him to escape safely. He could have at least warned me of the possibility of the mother returning home early. But then, so could Thia.

At that moment I didn't have time to question her, for all I could think was that I was up shits creek without a paddle. I had two options. One, to go downstairs, face Mama and die, or option two, jump out the second-floor window and hope I didn't get killed doing so. Facing Mama definitely was not an option, so I took the latter and jumped out of the window, clothes in hand. I couldn't help notice the neighbors watching my naked ass as I flew through the air as if on a trapeze. I landed safely and ran without missing a stride with the agility of a frightened man. The worst part about the whole situation was that this was the project where I lived and everybody knew me. People were on the ground laughing and rolling as if they were at a Richard Pryor concert.

I finally caught up with Hawkbeek who was waiting at the corner, and yes, that dirty motherfucker was dying laughing too. Mad and pissed off, I said to him, "Your day will come." After a couple of minutes had passed, I calmed down.   We started boasting about who fucked the pussy best, while deciding who would be our next victims.

The neighbors proved loyal to Ann and Thia, they never told on them. However, one of the mothers who saw my naked ass and swinging dick, later told me that if she ever caught me around her house or her daughters she would blow my ass to kingdom come.   All I could say was, "Yes ma'am."

Hawkbeek and I had been checking out two sisters who lived behind him.   They were not the most attractive girls but they would come in handy during a dry spell.   They agreed to meet us one Saturday at Hawkbeek's house just down the sidewalk from my house.   His mother was gone to work so we were home free to enjoy the pleasure.   This time he took his mother's bedroom and gave me his little dingy room.   But this time it didn't matter which room I got, there was pussy in both, and no one would show up unexpectedly.

We split off into our designated rooms that were across from each other, and without wasting any time, directed our attention to the girls.   I didn't spend a lot of time with foreplay on this chick since she wasn't the best looking and didn't have the greatest body.   Kissing her was out of the question, so to excite her I put my hand inside her bloomers and caressed her cunt.   She was very tight and not too wet. I could tell this girl was not having much sex, if any at all. But that was good because tight pussy is always good pussy. Having already undressed ourselves I laid her on the bed and pushed my big dick deep inside her.   In pain, she screamed over and over again, "I want my grandmama! I want my grandmama!" but she didn't want me to stop.

About that time I heard my boy next door moaning and talking out loud, "I'm gonna cum! I'm gonna cum!"

I then heard the girl, who had not made a sound up to that time, shout, "You can't cum now, you aren't even in!"

"It's not in?" asked Hawkbeek. "If it's not in, well, where is it?"

"It's down between my cheek and the sheet and you're cumming on my booty," she yelled in disgust.

By that time I was in tears, laughing so hard until my dick went limp. Still laughing I fell to the floor, crawled to the room where he was, stood up as I exposed my naked body and between laughter, said, "It's not in yet...it's down between my cheek and the sheet..." Before I could finish I fell to the floor again, laughing uncontrollably.

The girl was mad. For fifteen minutes he had been screwing the sheet and could not hold his cum, which was all over her buttocks and the bed.

Now the shoe was on the other foot. My boy got mad at me and acted as if he wanted to fight, but he knew he had no win there, so he asked me to get out of his house. Still laughing, I put on my clothes, looked at him and said, "Payback is a motherfucker."

That day, it didn't matter that I didn't bust my nut. I had more pleasure laughing about him fucking himself.

CHAPTER 6

PLEASURE AND PAIN

Well, Hawkbeek and I made up and were off doing our thing again; this time chasing after two old friends, Gila and Beth. The last time we were supposed to meet, Gila's mother decided that she would take her to school that day. I found out that Hawkbeek had no knowledge of the situation leading up to that time.

I had waited patiently for some time to get next to Gila. She was a very attractive girl, petite in stature, high-yellow skin, black hair, and dark, luminous eyes. Gila was the kind of girl you put on your layaway plan until your break came. She was from a large family with a lot of brothers and sisters. I knew her family because a few years prior they had lived in the project on the opposite side. Her mother was very strict so I knew sex with her would not be an easy task. I was aware that if I managed to make love to her, the times would be far between. So my plan was to bang her one good time and move on.

We were unable to arrange a setting for the four of us so we decided to pair off and get together whenever we could. Gila had informed me that she would be home alone on Saturday morning between 10 a.m. and 1 p.m. So that morning I went to her house one half hour early and waited across the street. I watched to make sure that everyone had left then went around to the back door where she was waiting for me. We went to her bedroom and talked for what seemed like an eternity.

After we got comfortable with each other we became affectionate. I undressed myself, and then Gila, kissing and touching her body after each piece of garment that I removed. She was truly tender and sweet, with very soft pubic hair that I loved playing with. I laid her on the bed and without hesitation, mounted her. She sighed and mumbled adulation about how good she was feeling; she dug her fingers deep into my back. Wrapping her legs around me, she climaxed joyfully. After allowing myself time to enjoy her to the fullest, I raised her legs high and repeatedly thrust my rod deep inside her. When she couldn't take anymore I exploded into her. Afterwards we talked for a while longer then realized that our time had all but expired. I cleaned up and left feeling good as the day.

Hawkbeek was spending time with Beth on occasion. How much time, I wasn't sure because I had been doing my own thing. I wasn't sure if he had gotten the drawers yet, but I knew that he cared for her. She was fairly good-looking, had a great body with a plump little ass. Now, decent-looking females with great bodies always got my attention. Beth had a great body and I had an itch that needed scratching. Given her great body, I wanted to fuck her myself.

Beth and I had talked several times in person and on the phone, and I could tell that she was interested in me. Knowing this didn't help, especially when I knew that I had no willpower for refusing sex.

Unlike Hawkbeek, I had the freedom to roam about the city. This made my meeting with Beth very easy, so we decided to slip away one Saturday to my brother's house where we spent about four hours making wild, good sex. I turned her ass every which way but loose.

Hawkbeek was unaware of what was going on with Beth and I, so we ducked and dodged until she felt the right thing to do was to be honest. Beth had decided that she wanted me and not him, and didn't want to play hide-and-seek any longer. I tried to tell her that honesty was not always the best policy. In this case it definitely was not. I didn't want her full-time and having my boy in the picture kept things simple. I knew she did not want me to be honest, because if so, her ass was about to be terminated. I didn't tell her to fall in love, I just told her when to fuck me. But I didn't want to end it because she could make a dick light up like a cigar, but seeing that she would be a problem, I ended it.

Talk about angry. Homegirl went straight to Hawkbeek and told him the whole story. She was shocked when Hawkbeek told her to get out of his face because I couldn't have gotten in her drawers unless she allowed me. I gave him praise that day. All he and I wanted to know was who was next!

Hawkbeek and I decided to go to the dance at Sixteen Street Junior High School to check out some new girls. The dance was crowded as usual and had a lot of new faces. While dancing, I collected names and phone numbers, which I added in my little black book. I would ask the girls several questions and based on their answers, I would place them into categories of easy, not so easy, and difficult. Naturally, the following week I called the easy ones first. For me that method was much better than spending all my time chasing after one girl and being seen doing so. That eliminated having to explain myself as I moved from victim to victim. Also, I refused to walk anybody home because that could destroy my chances with other girls if I was seen.

Now on the other hand, Hawkbeek decided to walk this little chick home. From the moment he laid eyes on her he chased her around the dance floor all night. She was built straight up-and-down. She was so small she could hide behind a pencil and not be seen, definitely not my type.

Both Hawkbeek and I had a curfew of eleven o'clock and eleven o'clock did not mean one minute after eleven, but 10:59 p.m. The dance was out at 10:30, so I told Hawkbeek that there was no way he could walk Lou-Lou home and make it home by curfew. But he insisted.

"It's your ass, not mine," I said, as I went on home. I reached home about 10:50 p.m., let my mother know I was home, and waited on the porch for Hawkbeek.

Around 11:15 p.m. his mother, Mrs. Mary, came to my house looking for her son. She was steaming mad. "Pookey, where is Hawkbeek?"

"He walked his new girlfriend home."

"What new girlfriend?"

"I don't know her name, but she's nice and attractive."

"Where does she live?"

"I think she lives on Melrose Avenue. He said he would make curfew so he should be home anytime," I said, scratching my head. "The girl seemed to be a decent young lady." I hoped to make an impression on Mrs. Mary.

"If she was decent, she wouldn't be out with him this time of night!"

When Mrs. Mary left, the expression on her face indicated that Hawkbeek was in deep shit.

About ten minutes later Hawkbeek came running up the sidewalk, dripping wet with sweat. Laughing, I told him he was in big trouble and that his mother was going to kick his ass. He ran home and I ran behind him. I sure wasn't going to miss seeing this thrashing. See, we enjoyed watching each other get our ass kicked, and that night, it was his turn.

Hawkbeek started crying before he went inside the house. I noticed that his Uncle Bubba was visiting, and hoped that was a good sign because his uncle had saved his butt before. Old Bubba was a drunk and only came around when he needed something.

The first thing Hawkbeek said was, "Mama, please don't kill me!"

I fell out laughing real hard. I couldn't make any noise because his mother would have kicked my ass too.

Mrs. Mary pulled out a razor strap and hit him real hard across the back. He screamed out in agony. Before she could hit him again he broke out in a sprint for the door. But guess what? Mama had locked the door, and there was nothing worse than running from Mama. She hit him again, and my boy screamed out, "Oh, Lord! Uncle Bubba, please don't let her kill me! Mama you told me I needed to get a girlfriend!"

I could no longer contain my laughter. I was so hysterical I fell on the grass kicking and rolling. That was the most fun I had had in a while. Unable to take my laughing any longer, Mrs. Mary came outside and swung at me but missed. I took off like a bat out of hell. You see, Mrs. Mary could outrun both Hawkbeek and me so I was scared she would run me down and beat the shit out of me.

The next day when I saw Hawkbeek I asked him if he was all right. He nodded his head indicating a yes. Apparently, his Uncle Bubba had stepped in and saved him after two more whips.

"Good," I said. Then I looked him in the eyes and playfully imitated him, "Oh, Lord! Uncle Bubba, please don't let..." I couldn't finish, I just fell out laughing. Well, Hawkbeek was on punishment for a while.

CHAPTER 7

THE TRAIN

I was hanging out at my friend Hickie's house, listening to Arthur Prysock's golden voice as he sang smooth love songs. Hickie was 6'0," very thin, and had a knot on each side of his forehead resembling that of Frankenstein. There was a knock at the door and in came this chick Hilary, wanting to know if she could chill with us for a while. Naturally, we said yes. Hilary lived down the street from Hickie and I noticed from time to time that she would show up at his house. She was average looking, light complexioned and athletically built. The word among the guys was that he was banging her.

She was always friendly with me at school, but on this day she was extremely friendly. Hickie didn't seem to be interested in what was going on nor did he seem concerned with her behavior, but since it was his house I wanted to give him the benefit of the doubt. I waited for a while to be absolutely certain that my feelings were correct.

"Hilary, excuse me, I need to speak to Hickie."

"Sure, go ahead."

"Hickie, I need some info."

"OK," he said.

"What's up with you and Hilary?"

"Nothing really. She's just a fuck thing."

"Why is she coming on to me?"

"You had mentioned in a prior conversation that you wanted to screw her so I set it up."

"I didn't want to disrespect you in your house so I thought it was best to check with you."

"No problem. I'm tired of that pussy anyway so go for the gusto."

"Thanks, man. I'm sure I'll return the favor one day," I said as I turned in the direction of Hilary.

"Hey, Baby, thanks for being patient," I said as I began to softly caress her hands, slowly moving up to her arms and shoulders. She responded with a smile and some touching of her own. I suggested that we go into the bedroom where we could have a little more privacy. Hickie, aware of what was going on gave me the nod to use the bedroom. We headed for the bed and wasted no time kissing and heavy petting.

After a short while I spread her legs and slid my penis deep inside her, watching and listening for sounds of passion. She was quiet and showed little emotion. For the first time I had been unable to cause pain on entry. She was different from all the rest, because I couldn't feel the walls of her vagina. That young girl was deep and wide. Somebody had already knocked the bottom out of her. Reaching a climax was almost impossible since there was no friction to my loins.

After two hours of banging in the bottomless pit with the persistence and the will to be the best, I finally made her cum, and then myself. After the longest sex escapade I had ever had, Hilary left. That was the only girl who didn't have to worry about me coming back for seconds. Knowing that Hickie had slept with Hilary on more than one occasion explained how this black hole came to be. Hickie was the only person in town that I knew of with a dick bigger than mine. I was a horse, but he was an elephant.

It was Wednesday afternoon and I had just finished eating lunch in the cafeteria. I went outside and joined Manny and Swet who had been rapping about the happenings around school. Things had been pretty dull with very little going on, so everyone was looking for some action. Manny and Swet informed me that one of the girls they knew gave them permission to come over to her house after school. They indicated that in addition to them, two other guys were going. The girl had agreed to let them pull a train on her. They wanted to know if I wanted to come along. Now for those of you who don't know what a train is, it's when a girl allows a group of guys to have sex with her, one after the other.

Normally, I would never go on trains and didn't enjoy that type of sex because it was unsafe. Also, in most situations like that the girl was usually less than good looking. I liked the challenge of conquering my prey's mind as much as I liked the sex. See, for me the chase was the excitement, the sex was the reward. I always gravitated toward the girls that no one else could get. However, easy girls filled up an awful lot of down time. So, on this given day, I decided to go along with the guys just for kicks, with no intentions of having sex.

All the fellows walked together to the girl's house, bickering amongst themselves as to who was on first. When we reached the house she was there waiting all alone. The guys were more excited than kids in a candy store. Manny, who was dark in complexion and rather short with pearl-white teeth and a stunning smile, as told by his admirers, was the first up and had come prepared. He pulled out a rubber, put it on and went humping nonstop, 90-miles-per-minute until he came; smiling and happy as a lark.

Swet, who was medium height and not bad looking was on next. Guiding his dick with both hands, he headed for the target. I noticed that he didn't have on a rubber so I asked him if he was going to screw her without protection. He said that he didn't have a rubber; he asked if anyone had any extras.

"Sorry, Swet, we just brought one," they replied.

Then, the most amazing thing happened. He asked Manny if he could borrow his rubber so he could fuck the girl. Scratching my head in confusion, I observed the girl who didn't seem to give a shit if a horse showed up and stuck his dick in her. The other dicks in line were getting pissed off because the dick in the batter's box was taking too long. Manny pulled off his rubber (full of cum) and gave it to him. Swet turned the rubber inside out and put it on his dick. Now, I'm looking at this shit and asking myself what the fuck am I missing? I was about to turn into a basket case.

Knowing all of the germs from the girl were now next to his skin, I said, "Swet, you might as well take off the rubber and fuck the bitch bare dick. Don't you know that when you turned the rubber inside out you put the germs from her on to you? If she's got something, it now belongs to you."

He looked at me and said, "Huh, what you talking about?"

Frustrated, I said, "You're good to go, do your thing." Either way it went he was either going to catch something from Manny or the girl. The expression on his face told the story of that good-fucking bitch.

Well, two bangers were out and the next dick was on deck. Dick #3 was as ugly as the pussy he was about to fuck. Tall, skinny, dark skinned, buck teeth, nappy hair, and blood-shot eyes, that dude was prepared and ready, his cock was hard and his protection was in place, no wasting time here. She was still lying there with legs open, inviting all partakers who were willing and brave enough to take part by hooking up to the train. The muscles of her pussy were throbbing, as if saying, all dicks aboard.

Then, the damndest thing happened. Dick #3 dropped to his knees and said, "I want to eat this pussy before I fuck her. Do ya'll think she will mind?"

I went fucking ballistic and said, "Hell no, she won't mind. Eat that motherfucker like it's fried chicken, bite that crusty bitch and eat till your ass gain weight." Unable to take anymore of their dumb shit I left in a hurry.

Guess what happened a few days later. If you can't figure out that Swet caught the claps, you are dumb as he was for turning the rubber inside and out, and dumber than the dummy who had oral sex with a girl who was trampled by a train. That was an original.

CHAPTER 8

LUST TO LOVE

It was now early in the year of 1967, and I was banging my neighbor who was a single parent with four children. I had always had a way with women, knowing what to say at the right time, and it surely paid off this time with an older woman. The good thing about older women is that you don't have to beg or play games to get them in bed. Either they are going to give it to you or they will just curse your ass out. I was seventeen years old and she was in her mid-thirties with a face that wore the pain of a woman who had struggled to survive.

The first time I went inside her house was early one Saturday morning while the kids were still asleep. She led me straight upstairs to her bedroom and locked the door. The layout of her apartment was the same as mine. She must have been starving for dick because she undressed me the second we entered the room. She didn't want any foreplay either.

"I just want this big, young dick," she said as she got into bed and pulled me down on top of her, grabbing my cock and guiding it straight to her vagina. She moaned softly. "I've been wanting this dick for such a long time," she expressed between moans.

Realizing that I was in another black hole, I was beginning to think she was Hilary's mother. I could tell that she was a smoker. As her body became heated, the smell of smoke radiated through her pores. One thing was for sure, I was definitely not going to kiss her. This was one of those times I was going to hit it 'n quit it. To my surprise she came quickly then started telling me to put all my cum in her. It's not easy to cum when you are pounding loose pussy, especially an old loose pussy. But I liked the feeling I got from making love and had no intentions of cumming early.

During my intense lovemaking I had failed to hear the noises coming from the kids' room. Upon her bringing this to my attention I put my ass on autopilot and came to her satisfaction. After I finished cumming I pulled out my dick and noticed that the pussy stayed open. This pussy had been in so many wars until none of the muscles worked, I thought. She put on a robe and went to the kids' room, keeping them inside to allow me to escape unseen. I had the feeling that this was my stuff to pound whenever I wanted to. I was thinking after I left that even bad pussy was good pussy when you didn't have pussy. So I decided to be nice and keep her available just in case I had a sexual drought.

Feeling very confident after conquering my neighbor I decided to take on another neighbor who lived next door to Hawkbeek named Velma. She was tall, super fine, had a radiant smile, and was good looking. Her sandy-brown hair and soft brown eyes complemented her white chocolate skin—a real knockout. She smoked, but with her fine self, all that was to be overlooked. Velma was also a single parent. She had three children and was about 15 years older than me. The good thing about the project was that it was designed for single mothers—my kind of place.

One day we were having one of our many football games in the field in front of my house; the oldest of her sons was playing with us since he was only two years younger than me. The other two smaller kids were outside playing children's games in front of the house. After waiting awhile for my big break, I decided to go to Velma's house and run my game. I had developed a big head, feeling very confident that I could have this woman. So, after she invited me in, we sat on the couch and started talking, having a general, semi-intimate conversation. Things were going according to plan.

While talking, I gradually kept moving closer to her. I was just about ready to try and kiss her when the door swung open. Standing in the doorway was her big, mean looking, six feet two inches, 230 pounds of muscle boyfriend with battle scars under both eyes. The type of marks you see on rugged football players. Standing with a hard, bulging dick was yours truly. Thinking that this man was going to kill me I started looking around in the direction of the back door because I was about to skedaddle. Everyone knew that this man was one of the baddest dudes in town.

Sensing that I was about to make a dash for the back door, he shouted, "Don't move!"

I instantly froze, as he stood motionless. I guess he was trying to figure out what in the hell was going on and what he was going to do about it. He finally spoke. "Get your punk-ass out of here and don't ever let me catch you in here again." I didn't say a word, just got out of there in a flash. I never set foot in that house again.

One night I was at a weekly dance at the Topper club. The DJ had it going on and everyone was having a great time. For some reason my partners in sex crimes didn't show up that night, so I was solo, checking out the girls. I had my eyes on two young ladies who seemed to be hanging together. One of the sweeties name was Doria. I had seen her at the dance before. I didn't know the other sweetie, but I would before the night was over. I had had my eyes on young, fine Doria for quite some time. She was petite in stature with a firm, plump little ass. What I admired was the way she switched that ass when she walked. I liked Doria, but then, I also liked her friend. I decided that I would focus my attention on Doria tonight. However, I would see if I could get a phone number from the other chick and then call her at a later date. For now, it was Doria time.

I watched as she danced around, slinging her little booty all over the place to the #1 hit song by Aretha Franklin, *R-E-S-P-E-C-T*. She had my attention and I was hungry for her love. I moved into position while waiting for the disc jockey to play a slow jam. But as you know they play one slow record for every five fast ones, so I had to hold my position. The next song was a fast one but I decided to dance, hoping the song after would be slow. That way she would already be in my arms. I grabbed her hand to signal that I wanted to dance. She swung herself around, dancing without missing a beat. The next song was a slow jam and I pulled her close to me, placing my arms firmly around her body. She responded by holding me tightly.

"I like the way you dance," I said.

"Thank you."

"I've been admiring you for quite some time."

"You have?" she said.

"Yes, I have."

"Why?"

"Because I like what I see."

"And what is that?"

"Your smile, your body, and the way you carry yourself," I whispered, as I pulled her closer to me.

"Is that right."

"Yes, that's right and because it's right, I'd like to get to know you better. Are you seeing anyone?"

"Yes, but he's not around at this time," she replied.

I took that as a no. The last song of the evening was a slow one and I grabbed her one last time. This time she squeezed me passionately while moving her body in perfect sync with mine.

After the dance, I asked if I could walk her home—she said yes. Generally, I did not walk anyone home because it alerted everyone as to whom I was dating or attempting to date, but Doria lived in my neighborhood just across the alley from the project. I knew no one would suspect anything out of the norm since we all usually walked the same way home.

We arrived at her house around 10:45 p.m., talked for a few minutes, and then I left. I had to be home by 11:00, and my mother didn't take any excuses short of death. That night I slept soundly because I had a good feeling about Doria. She was going to be mine, regardless. The next day I went over to her house but felt uncomfortable as her aunt, uncle, and cousins were all in the room with us. I made a point to see her every day for a little while, just to let her know that I cared for her; and I really did. Doria was special and I felt good when we were together. We had a lot of fun, laughing, teasing—just talking about everything.

The following Friday night I went to her house. Things were different since no one was in the living room with us, and when alone, I was always at my best. Her older cousin was with her boyfriend in the bedroom adjacent to us. Doria and I had reached a point in our relationship of kissing passionately. While kissing, I would caress her breasts and thighs, but every time I would make an attempt to put my hand inside her panties, she would grab it while continuing to kiss me. Whenever she held my hand I would move it down toward my crotch so that she could feel the hard surprise that awaited her. She acknowledged with a smile and a sigh of appreciation.

I knew that becoming intimate would take some time, and I was patient because I was still fucking my neighbor whenever I chose to. I had all my bases covered and loving every minute. I was good because I could out think and manipulate anyone at any time. The key to scoring with Doria was to make and keep her thinking that she was more important than the sex. It just so happened that in this case she was, and that was a rarity for me. Never before had caring about someone superseded sex. Was I starting to go soft or what?

One day I went to Doria's house and saw that her face and body had swollen out of proportion. She didn't look anything like herself, which was quite scary. I told her she looked like she had the hebe-jebees. What the hell that was, I didn't know, but ugly as she was she looked like something from the unknown.

Later I learned that she had eaten some crabs that were cooked with cayenne pepper. Whenever I wanted to aggravate her I would call her hebe-jebee, but by now I could do no wrong. It took about one week for her to get better. I was glad to see her looking like her old self again.

On a Saturday night in April 1967, during the beginning of spring, I was on the way to my baby's house with sex on my mind. When I got there we went upstairs to our favorite little cozy room. No one was in the house but us. We started kissing and touching each other, enjoying every second as if we had a lifetime—this was our moment. She was kissing me passionately in a way she had not done before. I moved her down to a lying position on the couch, while still kissing her. I lifted her blouse to fondle her breasts, which were firm, the nipples erected. My mouth was full with her tongue inside. I gently proceeded down toward her breasts, lightly sucking on her nipples, one after the other. With my hand inside her panties, I rubbed her clitoris with light, easy strokes, she moaned with a smile. Her lips were dry, so she moistened them with her saliva. I moved my mouth from her breasts and kissed her hard. My finger was deep within her, moving in and out, touching her clitoris with each stroke.

I could tell she was experiencing being finger fucked like she had never before encountered. She was moist, wet all over with passion. I removed her panties while licking her breasts then pushed my fingers back inside her saturated cunt. She didn't resist even if she had wanted to. Her heart, body, and soul belonged to me. I moved my body on top of her and spread her legs all in one motion. Raising my head to get a clear view of her expressions, I slid myself deep inside her. She moaned loudly and made strange sounds as if speaking in tongue. We were good together and our rhythm was in tune.

In the middle of our brief love session, I heard sounds coming from the hallway. Someone was approaching. I quickly sat up and covered myself with the only thing available, a magazine. There was no time to put my dripping wet penis back in my pants. I pulled Doria's dress down to cover herself, as she lay in the same position, moaning softly as if I was still inside her. She had gone to heaven without dying. Thank God it was only her little cousin, and not her aunt or uncle.

It was quick, too quick. But that was all right because she was mine and there would be many more times, I thought. I couldn't have been more confident.

Over the next couple of months we spent a lot of time together but had very little time alone. However, we took advantage of every situation, in spite of her aunt and uncle's suspicion of our sexual involvement.

CHAPTER 9

WHO'S THE FATHER?

It was late May 1967 and summer vacation was almost here. Doria was sick with flu-like symptoms and had been throwing-up on and off for awhile. We had planned to go to the sock-hop dance, but she was too sick so I went alone. At the dance I met Doria's friend Dell, who had also come to the dance alone. Dell was the other little sweetie I'd seen that night with Doria. I approached her and started a casual conversation. I was very careful not to discuss anything too personal.

In a sly way, I was trying to get her testimony on her friendship with Doria. The trick was to get her to think that I was interested in her without me actually saying so. If I didn't say it, she couldn't tell it. And if she liked me, she would definitely let me know. All's fair in the game of love. I was disappointed when she said she was interested in some other person so I didn't push it.

During a hot day in early June, I went by Doria's house but no one answered the door, so I walked toward Harden's grocery store. About halfway there I saw Doria's aunt; she stopped me.

A real shady lady with short hair, blood-shot eyes and parched lips from her constant drinking, she informed me that Doria was pregnant and that I didn't have to worry because the baby wasn't mine. I stood there silent and numb. Sadness fell upon me like a dark cloud. I was hurting and very confused. I didn't know whether to shit or go blind. I was thinking about all the times I had spent upstairs with

Doria—when in the hell did she sleep with someone else, and who the hell was the son of a bitch!

Boy was I mad. My eyes were stinging from the tears that I was trying very hard not to let flow. I could not afford to be seen like this. I was miserable. All I could think about was that she better have something real good to tell me, or I was going to kick her ass.

Every day for the next few days I went to her house, attempting to see her, but without success. One day I stopped in for a haircut at the barber shop that was located downstairs on the corner of the same building that Doria lived in. The two barbers were talking about her being pregnant. The owner of the shop insinuated that she was pregnant by me as he was aware that she was taking my company. I sat motionless, listening without saying a word, feeling bad enough as it was. I didn't need anyone hassling me because if I got angry I would do or say something out of the ordinary. So, after I got my haircut I left, mad as hell and feeling like I wanted to hurt somebody.

Finally, after two weeks of constant attempts I got to see her. She looked very sad. I could tell she had been crying because her eyes were puffy and red. At that moment, all the anger I was feeling subsided. The good in me was greater than the evil. Instead of wanting to hurt her, I wanted to hug and squeeze her, just to let her know that everything would be all right. I felt sorry for her, she was only fifteen years old and I knew times would be difficult. I told her what her aunt had said then asked if I was the father. She paused; tears started flowing from her eyes like someone had turned on a faucet. Still not answering, I asked her again. With her head hung down, afraid to look me in the eyes, she said, "No, and don't worry about it."

With my eyes filled with tears I assured her that if the baby was mine I would do my part. She repeated herself saying, "No, and don't worry about it," then walked off without providing me with any information as to who the father was. I stood there stunned, feeling as if the darkess of days were upon me. I didn't have a clue as to what was happening. All I knew was that I really cared for her and now she was having someone else's baby. For the next few weeks I walked around like a zombie, not going anywhere or visiting anyone.

Things were different with Doria. Whenever I had finished my business with the other girls I was ready to leave, but this time, I wanted to stay, but couldn't.

We were three weeks away from the start of my senior year and football practice was in session. I was truly looking forward to its start as I needed something to ease the pain I was feeling.

I was one of the superstar players on the team. I had earned the school letter in my junior year. Everyone including myself expected great things from me. Most of my friends, Hawkbeek, Manny, and Swet were on the team. During pre-season practice there was little time for girls. After practicing three times a day, there was little energy left to chase after girls. Over the next few weeks we worked very hard getting conditioned for our first game.

As a result of integration, we participated for the first time in the white conference. New civil rights laws, specifically integration, made it possible for black students to attend white schools and compete against the white athletes. Except for personal goals, competing against white competitors highly motivated me to be the best that I could be.

Every once in awhile I would visit Doria, assuring her that everything would turn out just fine, but whenever I brought up the subject of the baby or the baby's father, she would quickly end the conversation and subsequently my visit. I started hearing bits and pieces of information around the neighborhood as to the father of her child. Her aunt had made statements that the father of the baby was the barber, not the owner, but his brother. Both barbers denied the allegations. They jointly persisted that neither of them had any sexual encounters with her and that she was pregnant by me. I had no way of validating who the father was, but I knew that the barbers had every reason to deny the accusations given their ages. They were over twenty-one years of age and would have been crazy to risk statutory rape. None of what was going on made sense to me, but Doria stuck to her story.

Every now and then I would visit her mother, attempting to gain insight as to why Doria had taken this position. She couldn't tell me much more than I already knew. She wasn't privy to Doria's master plan. Doria had to know that help and the child's father were just around the corner. I told her so myself. Why was she so secretive?

CHAPTER 10

FALLING IN LOVE

School started and I was looking foward to my senior year. Everyone seemed to be excited about being back in school after a long, hot summer. Football season was in session and the team was doing quite well. As for myself I was doing excellent, playing up to and sometimes above expectations. Prior to one of our games, one of my teachers promised me $10 for each pass I caught. That Monday in class he had to fork over $40. That week he refused to make a pledge; he said he couldn't afford me on a teacher's salary.

I had not forgotten Doria, but she was definitely out of my system as a result of her circumstances and her position on the baby issue; however, I wouldn't stop trying to get to the bottom of her situation. I had to know who and why.

It was a beautiful October morning and all the students were making their way to class. Some of the football players, including myself, usually stood at the front entrance to the building scrutinizing the girls as they made their way to class. On this particular day we wore our football jerseys, which gave us the edge. Girls wanted to date football players.

As I scanned the crowd for one last look before going to class, my eyes focused on the most beautiful girl I had ever seen. She was average height with nicely shaped C-cup breasts, a small waist, and shapely hips that formed her petite body.

Her hair was as black as coal and she had dark, sexy, slanted-eyes plugging into her bright coppertone face accentuated by her plump, lusciously soft lips. What a goddess, I thought. Without hesitation, I moved directly in her path. After giving her my staredown from head to toe, I said, "Hello, I'm Johnny, what's your name?"

"My name is Chinadoll and I know who you are."

I was in hog heaven, I thought, as I opened the door for her, like gentlemen do, and watched her until she disappeared into the building. I knew she was the one I wanted to spend the rest of my life with; there was no doubt. Eternity was all that I desired, as my heart, body and soul fell prey to the mystic of her beauty. I walked over to my friends and told them that she was mine.

"Don't even think about trying to talk to her," I threatened as I walked away.

That day I found out that her brother was in my class. I told him to let her know that I wanted to talk to her. The next day I asked him if he had given his sister the message and he said yes. Anxious to hear her reply I asked, "What did she say?"

He hesitated for a while then said, "You can talk," and gave me the phone number.

That night I called her and we talked for about an hour. I could tell from our conversation that she enjoyed talking to me as much as I enjoyed talking to her. I listened attentively and made sure I said all the right things.

The next morning I waited for her in front of the school, and like clockwork, she showed up right on time. I smiled, complimented her on how good she looked and how much I enjoyed our conversation the night before then proceeded to walk her to class while making small talk. All my friends who were standing outside and witnessed me in action were very impressed with how cool I was, and the fact that I told them that she would be mine. I was as happy as a pig in slop.

Everyone was afraid to talk to her because no one thought they had a chance. But I was always at my best when the odds were against me.

For the rest of the week Chinadoll and I talked every night after I got home from football practice, and every morning we met in front of the school and walked to class together. In the past my success rate had been dependent on camouflage, but now, I didn't care who saw me with Chinadoll. I had the girl of my dreams. My diamond in the rough, I was in love! I must admit, it felt good not having to duck and dodge anymore.

The following Saturday I went to her house for the first time to visit. She lived in a two-story house with a steep gable on the front. The front door opened directly into a large great room with a fireplace at the far end opposite the front door. Immediately to the left of the entry was an arch opening leading to a formal dining room. The kitchen was beyond the dining room and had a door for side entry. Off from the kitchen was a guest room. Halfway from the great room was a set of stairs leading to the three bedrooms and bathroom on the second floor. Just past the stairs was a small hallway allowing access to the first-floor bathroom.

When I arrived Chinadoll was home alone. We sat on the couch across from the stairs. I saw another couch on the wall adjacent the bathroom. There was a coffee table in the center of the room with two easy chairs, one located next to the front door and the other, to the right of the fireplace.

After making myself comfortable we started talking, discussing many issues including whether or not I was the father of Doria's baby. But now I was happy Doria said the baby wasn't mine because I didn't want anything or anyone to interfere with my relationship with Chinadoll. She was my soul mate. I told her I was positive I wasn't the father. To reassure her some more I decided to tell her the whole story as I knew it, just in case someone decided to tell a different story. But then who knew better than I, except Doria, and she wasn't talking. Chinadoll seemed very satisfied with my answer. At that point we moved the conversation to a more intimate topic.

I didn't want her to think that I had sex on my mind so I was careful not to be too aggressive. I saw her as a nice young lady who was brought up with good values. I was sure she had been taught what to watch out for, so I decided to follow her lead. We kissed passionately; pausing for brief conversation then repeated the sequence. Her lips were soft and sweet, and I was becoming addicted to them. A great kisser she was.

Our moment of passion was interrupted when we heard the kitchen door being unlocked. At first we thought it was her brother but to our surprise her dad walked in. His attire was impressive, and the wide brim hat on his head completed his get up to a "T." He had a unique walk, as if one leg was slightly longer than the other. Judging from his grimaced expression I wasn't sure if he thought more was going on than what met his eyes. The room was dimly lit by only the light entering through the glass at the front door. The curtains at the windows were still drawn from the night before. At that moment I felt a little nervous.

He called her into the kitchen, spoke to her briefly then went upstairs. When she returned she said that she had to complete her chores, so I kissed her lightly on the lips and left.

About twenty yards from the house a green station wagon matching the paint on Chinadoll's house pulled up beside me. It was her father. My nervousness turned to fear, especially when he called me to the car and I saw his gun lying on his lap.

"Do you plan to continue seeing my daughter?" he asked.

"Yes, sir."

Picking up his gun in his right hand he then said in a deep, mean voice, "No one else will be coming to my house as long as you are coming, that way there won't be no confusion if my daughter was to get pregnant. If she gets pregnant, you will take care of her and the baby. Do you understand?"

"Yes, sir," I said nervously.

At that moment I was about to shit in my pants. I didn't know whether to cut my dick off or just not go back. I was wondering if she was really worth all that because I knew there was easier stuff out there. But as quickly as the thought entered my mind, it vanished. This was the love of my life and I was in for the long haul.

When I got home that night I called her and we talked for about three hours. She assured me that everything was all right with her father. I told her that he was all right with her because he didn't have his gun to her head. She laughed.

The next few weeks were the same routine. Talking on the phone at night after football practice and going to her house on Saturday and Sunday nights.

All the football games, except Homecoming, were played on a Friday. After the game Chinadoll would meet me at the locker room and I would walk her home. That was a special occasion for us as it afforded us the opportunity to be alone, if only for thirty minutes, without the watchful eyes of her parents.

Chinadoll always got a kick out of me saying something funny or stupid. She would often say, "Boy you are a fool!" I thought it couldn't get any better than that.

We had been going together for about two months when we decided that we were ready to take our relationship a step further by becoming more intimate.

She mentioned that she was not on any protection as she had never had intercourse. I told her that I spent a lot of time reading articles and books dealing with sex and had discovered that the rhythm method as a way to prevent pregnancy would be the best method for us. I told her that we would keep a close watch on her monthly cycle and after the tenth day following the start of her cycle I'd make sure I didn't ejaculate in her. My plan was to go to college in the fall while she continued her high school education. Upon graduating in four years with a degree in mathematics I would be prepared to get married, have children, get a house, a dog, and a white picket fence and live happily ever after.

We agreed that the following Saturday would be the magical day for us to go to my brother's apartment and spend the afternoon together. I talked to my brother to get clearance to use his apartment but he said he had plans of his own. I was ready to die.

My first chance of making love to the most precious girl in the world and my only brother told me that he had plans of his own. I told him that was totally unacceptable. The woman he was hitting was at best average looking so I figured he could lay her any time. It wasn't like she had a lot of men knocking at her door. What I really couldn't understand was that my brother was very handsome, but he seemed to gravitate toward the not so pretty—not to sound too drastic. I begged and begged mercifully, but he still said no.

"I'm going to tell Mama," I retaliated. Of course we both started laughing.

"I don't care what you tell Mama," he said between laughter.

So now my only other option was to be diplomatic so I said, "You know what it's like the first time and being a kid with no place of my own; I won't have many more chances."

He looked at me in a funny way and said, "I thought the time I gave you the French tickler was the first time, liar!"

"Oh, shit," was the only thing I could say. I had completely forgotten about that incident.

I begged again and again, letting him know I only needed it between 1 and 5 p.m. He looked at me very skeptical then finally said yes. I was back in business.

On Saturday, Chinadoll rose early to get an early start on her chores. I arrived at her house about 12:30 p.m. and we proceeded to my brother's crib for what I projected would be the most exciting and anticipated sexual experience I would ever have. It was early November and the temperature was in the mid-50s, cold for someone born and raised in Florida. We arrived about 12:50 p.m. I unlocked the door and we went inside.

My brother's apartment was set behind the main house on the right side. The inside was one large room with a closet and bathroom on the right side. The room was furnished with a stereo and television adjacent the wall between the bathroom and closet. The bed on the opposite wall was perpendicular to the door. A 2- by 4-foot tall window was next to the bed with a mirrored dresser in the corner next to the window.

For this lady, I wanted the mood setting to be perfect. The curtains were already drawn, making the room somewhat dark, allowing enough light for one to witness my heart pounding from the glow of her magnificent beauty. My brother was a jazz connoisseur so I put on Jimmy Smith, and my all time favorite, Wes Montgomery.

I stood behind Chinadoll, facing the mirror, observing the spirit of true love as it rose out of the image of the reflection. Turning her, never letting go, I kissed her passionately. After a short while I started removing her clothes; item for item, pausing every so often to admire the view while kissing softly on her nipples. She stood naked, bearing all, except her vaginal area. Slowly I pulled down her lace underwear, kissing her stomach as she watched in delight.

"I like that," she said as she undressed me in the same manner duplicating my every move. I lifted her, carrying her to the bed, hoping to make our love immortal. The room was quite cool so I pulled the covers up to our shoulders.

"I like looking at you," I said, while running my finger through her hair.

"Why?"

"Because you have very sexy eyes."

"You're sweet," she said smiling.

"I want you to know that this is more to me than just sex, it's an expression of my external love. I love you very much."

"I love you too. Please don't hurt me," she whispered, as tears flowed from her eyes.

"I won't hurt you. Are you all right?"

"Yes, it's just that I care so much for you. I'm scared of losing you."

Pulling her closer to me I said, "Baby, you don't have to worry about that, you are the love of my life."

"Do you really mean that?"

"What do you think?" I said, kissing her passionately while rubbing softly over her breasts and nipples. I started sucking lightly and licking on her nipples while caressing her thighs and pubes. I made every effort not to touch her vagina, I continued touching her until she began to moan. She was jubilant.

She took my hand in an effort to force me to feel directly between her legs. I refused to allow her to achieve satisfaction on her terms; it had to be on mine. I kissed her belly button—licking in circular motions, moving again to her breasts then down to her thighs and behind her knees, which was one of her sensitive spots. She was in a state of pure ecstasy, begging me to give it to her.

"I can't stand it, please give it to me," she said. "Oh, Pookey, please Pookey put it in," she moaned.

I opened her legs wider and played with her clitoris while kissing and sucking on her nipples. Feeling the juices flowing from between her legs in a steady stream, I sensed that she was ready so I gently inserted myself deep inside her, fucking her easily with long, deep strokes. She responded by moving her hips and clenched her legs around me.

"Is it good to you?" I asked.

"Oh, yes!"

"Do you like this dick?"

"Awwww Baby, Baby, I love this dick!"

Watching her every expression, I timed myself making sure I would be at my highest peak when she reached hers. I could feel myself getting harder.

"You going to cum for me?"

"Oh, yes! Oh, shit! This pussy is ready to cum."

"Give it to me. Wet this dick."

She moaned louder as she felt my cock growing inside her. Tears ran down her cheeks, she screamed aloud in bliss, "I'm there. Oh, my God! Pookey, I'm cumming."

Then I cried out "Oh, Chinadoll, this pussy is so good, I'm cumming with you. Oh, Baby it's so damn good!" Together we came as one.

Covered with sweat, we held each other tightly while our juices united. She smiled, looked at me with her beautiful oriental-shaped eyes and said, "I love you."

I smiled and said, "I love you back."

Still clenched together, she listened as I assured her that her love and passion would be cherished forever, that this was the beginning of our lifetime. At that moment my heart opened for the first time, allowing her to dwell internally, as she brought serenity to the unduress of a dick-born whore.

This was her first time and she was in obvious pain after the enjoyable feeling. So for the rest of our time I held her tightly, stroking her hair while kissing her softly, never once allowing her to feel regretful. Together, there and then we pledged our undying love.

The time was approaching 4:30 p.m. As we showered together for the first time, we took turns bathing each other.

My brother and his friend were coming in the driveway as we were leaving. She tried to hide to keep us from seeing her. I was thinking, if she's that ugly she should only come out at night with the rest of the creatures. I took a last glance to get a clear view of what she looked like. She may not have been pretty, but goddamn she was fine. I was so caught up with her finest that Chinadoll had to yank my head to keep me from walking into a light pole.

Now I understood. I learned something from my big brother. When the room is dark and heat builds up in the loins, they all look good. My dick gave her a nod of appreciation.

CHAPTER 11

JOY AND PAIN

The Homecoming game was a week away and the football team was preparing for the big game against Lakewood High School. Chinadoll was having a leather pants suit made to wear to the game, blue and gold to match the school colors.

During the week before the game I made every effort not to get sexually involved. Coach had convinced the players that sex before a game would take away our strength. I couldn't afford to let that happen.

Finally, it was game day. We had to be at school by 2 p.m to eat dinner so I was unable to see Chinadoll earlier that day. However, to my surprise, she stopped by the locker room prior to the game to see me, and to show off her new outfit. And boy, she was gorgeous.

The Homecoming game was a success. We won the game in a big way. I caught four passes, including one touchdown, kicked two extra points while on offense, and made lots of solo tackles and had one interception while on defense. With all that, I was selected player of the game. Each week the player of the game received a gift certificate to Frishe's Big Boy for a free hamburger, fries and Coke.

Unknown to anyone, I played the second half of the game in tremendous pain. During the third quarter while playing defense I read a pass play and put a real hard hit on the receiver for no gain. That's when I felt something pull on my right side. I was afraid that the coach would take me out of the game if he knew how I felt so I decided to just bear the pain and play the game.

After the match I could barely walk, but I found the strength to walk my baby home. I tried not to let her know how hurt I really was.

As the pain didn't get any less during the following week I was unable to play in the game that Friday. All during the game I pleaded with the coach to put me in, but he refused. The next week I practiced in pain while telling my coaches I was ready to play. This was our final game of the season, there was no way I would miss the last game. During the pre-game warm up I was worried because I knew that I was not near being ready, but I put on a good show. I guess my heart was stronger than my pain.

In the first quarter we had a first down and ten on our own three-yard line. The quarterback called the play, slot right seventy one roll-out. This play was designed for me only. The ball was snapped, I went down five yards and across the middle, caught the ball and ran 97 yards for a touchdown. That put my team ahead 7-0, a new school record.

Once again, during the play, something on my right side pulled and it was more painful than before. I could barely walk and was in excruciating pain but continued to play. In the second quarter I threw a block and was hit in the side by someone's knee, I could not get to my feet. I crawled to the sideline and told the coach to send in my replacement. That meant as many as six people would have to be substituted since I played on every team. After the game I got a ride home with Chinadoll to her house, stayed for a few minutes then walked home, which was just around the corner.

The next day I went to the team doctor and he said that I had pulled a muscle on my side and told me to keep a heating pad on it. I did as instructed hoping that everything would be all right.

The Thanksgiving holidays were upon us and Chinadoll invited me to have Thanksgiving dinner with her family. But I said no because all I could think about was sitting across from her dad while wondering if he had his gun under the table. My nerves and my fear of eating at someone else's house attributed to my being uncomfortable. I had dinner with my family, but later spent the evening with Chinadoll.

During the Thanksgiving holiday my neighbor approached me as to why I hadn't been spending time with her. She made it clear that she was horny and needed some attention at once. I told her that I was dating someone at my school and had ended all outside relationships. She got very angry and shouted, "When you needed to get your rocks off I was there for you, so why can't you be there for me?" I told her nicely that she should find a boyfriend in her own age group, someone that could help her. That really pissed her off even more. So I just said, "Sorry, I have no more dick for the weary." I then left her standing there, never to go her way again.

One thing was for sure, when it came to Chinadoll I was not going to fuck things up. On her birthday I decided to take her to the movies. She had asked her father if I could use the car to take her out on that special day. He was crazy about her, there was no way he was going to say no. We got the ride. We always tried to catch the 7 p.m. movie so we could have some time alone before our 11 p.m. curfew. After the movie I drove to one of my favorite little secluded spots.

Knowing my plan and how I wanted the night to go, I suggested that she wear a dress. We got in the back seat and I began to kiss her. I lifted her dress and took off her drawers, and immediately lowered my pants below the knees. I then positioned her in the best way possible, given that the back seat of a car is not the most ideal place for making love.

Pulling her outer leg toward me, I pushed myself deep inside her, moving in then out, feeling her body working against mine. She gasped as if choking, then moaned and kissed me, letting me know that she was about to cum. I slowed my rhythm, trying to prolong the feeling as well as the sensation she was getting. But she continued to move on me with rhythmic motions until she could no longer maintain herself, and I the same. We burst in ecstasy until all our hot juices mixed together like a tropical punch. We immersed in the love sweat of each other in the tiny back seat. Thinking ahead, I always made sure I brought along a small towel or at least some napkins from the theater to clean up with.

***

Christmas was approaching and I was wondering what to give Chinadoll on that special day. Every chance I got I would catch the bus downtown or to Central Plaza to look for the perfect gift. I could tell right away that this was not going to be easy. I had never bought a gift for anyone in the past so I hadn't the faintest idea what was fitting for the occasion.

Listening to my sisters make comments about what they wanted for Christmas helped. I decided to get her a sweater. I took the bus downtown to Maas Brothers department store where I found the most beautiful sweater. On Christmas day I went to her house early. We exchanged gifts, and like me she had bought a sweater, gold cashmere which was very nice. I stayed with her until her family sat down for dinner, then left to have dinner with my family.

After dinner I went back over to Chinadoll's. She had a grandmother staying with her who was not friendly but she made the best brownies I had ever tasted. For that reason, I looked foward to seeing her each holiday.

Chinadoll made me aware that some guy from school had been calling her.

"I asked him not to call anymore," she said.

"Do I need to get involved?" I asked.

"No, I have everything under control," she replied with a smile.

By now her father really liked me. I was mannerable and respected his every wishes pertaining to his daughter. He felt comfortable with me using the car, something he didn't allow his own son to do. I don't think they got along very well, if at all. Chinadoll's father was a real womanizer and a rebel, and so was I. I think he saw me in his own image.

CHAPTER 12

CLOSE CALLS

In late January news had spread that Doria had just given birth. It was a boy. A few days later I heard that she and the baby were discharged from the hospital and were staying with her mother in the project. Upon hearing that, I decided to pay her a visit.

The baby was sleeping when I got there. Naturally, I observed him to see if he looked like me. To be honest, I couldn't tell. He just looked like a baby.

I looked Doria straight in the eyes and asked, "Is this my son?"

Appearing nervous she said, "No, he is not your son so just leave it alone." I left, feeling unhurt.

A few weeks later my mother and I were in the kitchen and we saw Doria coming down the sidewalk, which was perpendicular to our house. Hearing talks about the baby, my mother had questioned me as to whether or not the child was mine. She made it very clear that if she found out that the child was mine I would support it. She had raised six children on her own without any help from our father and in no way was she going to stand by and watch me neglect my responsibility. But all I could tell her was what I had been told by Doria. So my mother called her and inquired if the child was mine. She told her if it was, I would take care of it.

"No, the child is not Pookey's. I wish everyone would leave me alone," she replied, almost screaming.

"As you wish, I just wanted to hear the truth from you," my mother said.

My birthday was just around the corner and Chinadoll asked me what I wanted for a present. "You, hot and juicy with nothing on," I replied.

She smiled and said, "The pleasure is all mine, consider it done."

On Saturday night I went over to her house as usual. Her father was out, customarily returning home about 10 p.m. Her mother never went anywhere and habitually went to bed around 9 p.m. We spent a lot of time talking, touching and kissing; avoiding sexual intercourse until after her father got home and went to bed.

Like clockwork her father came home at 10:00, said hello, and went straight upstairs to bed; usually never returning downstairs. After about fifteen minutes when everyone appeared to be settled, Chinadoll went upstairs to do a last minute check and to get a towel. We spread the towel on the couch so we wouldn't get any semen on it. She sat on the towel and lay back, allowing me to run my fingers up and down her clitoris. She moaned then licked her lips as if her mouth was dry. I lifted her pajama top just above her breasts and kissed on her stomach around the belly button, then kissed upward until I reached her nipples.

She was moaning and telling me how badly she wanted me. I took her tongue deep into my mouth then gave her mine to suck on. With my shoes already off and my pants unzipped, I pulled my pants down, enough to remove my penis with ease. Still begging me to give it to her I spread her legs and entered her already wet cunt.

We were both working it real good and Chinadoll was locked on, like a broken record saying, "Oh yes, it's good...oh yes, it's good." It seemed like each time she mumbled those words it got louder. Just as we were about to cum we heard someone rushing down the stairs. I quickly sat up and put the pillow that she always kept with her over my long, stiff dick. She only had time to move her inside leg but not enough time to sit up. At the bottom of the stairs appeared her dad. He stopped. I was more nervous than a chicken on a chopping block; my dick was so scared it backed up in my nuts. I checked his right hand to see if he had his gun. I was dead for sure.

He looked at us then asked if we were all right. We quickly responded. She said, "Yes, daddy" and I said, "Yes, sir." I was thinking, everything is all right as long as you don't ask me to move this pillow or stand up. I was praying, Lord please just let this man go back upstairs. My prayers were answered as he turned and ascended the stairs. But it didn't matter because my body was in shock from my brain to my dick. Nothing was working anymore.

"Are you ready to finish?" Chinadoll asked between laughs.

"Hell no! I'm limber as a dishrag."

"I need to cum," she continued.

"If you didn't cum before your dad came downstairs, you can cum when I come again and it will not be tonight," I said, as I made way for the door. "Goodbye!"

She was still laughing when I left but I didn't care.

***

The County Fair was in town and I planned to take Chinadoll on the weekend. We decided to go on Saturday so I borrowed the car and off we went. Her younger brother came with us since I liked him and he thought the world of me. Now the older brother was a different story all together. I don't think that he liked himself…strange.

At the fair that day I wanted desperately to win Chinadoll a nice prize so I took a shot at the game I played best, basketball. On my first attempt, I scored three baskets in a row. That won her the biggest prize they offered. She picked a bear. On my second try I made three more shots in a row and she got to pick another prize. There was a girl standing next to us and she asked if I would win her a nice prize and I did. Chinadoll was very happy and proud of me. After winning the prize for the girl, the attendant wouldn't allow me to shoot anymore hoops.

Chinadoll took home lots of prizes that day. She kept them all on her bed so she could hold them when I wasn't around. Her little brother had fun, but I don't think he won anything; he only had money for a hot dog.

***

Springtime came, a time when hormones are raging. Chinadoll had just informed me that her monthly was late. I really couldn't understand this because I was a master at the rhythm method and had watched the days very closely. Now I was scared and every day that went by without the red devil showing up was a nightmare for me. Memories of that first day I met her father, hearing his words and seeing that big gun in his right hand kept haunting me. Thoughts of going to college, receiving scholarships and all other things that a young man is supposed to do were now in jeopardy. If I went to college I wouldn't be able to work and make enough money to take care of a baby, so I was dead. At least, if I gave up college, the football scholarships, and worked like a dog to take care of my responsibility, I would still be alive. Hurray, big fucking deal.

Every day I got a report from Chinadoll as to her condition. I found myself worrying more about her than myself. I quickly realized that I loved her so much nothing could be so bad, as long as we were together. Even though my college education was important, it wasn't as important as her finishing high school. I prepared myself for the sacrifice and was determined that she would complete high school after having the baby, if I wasn't dead.

A couple of weeks went by and I noticed that nothing could sexually arouse me. That was virtually impossible. But then, I had flashbacks of her dad with the gun. I knew that was to be blamed for my short-term impotency.

By Wednesday morning I hadn't seen my girlfriend yet, that was strange because we usually saw each other before our first class. About 11 a.m. on my way to physics class I met her in the hall. She was smiling, showing all 32 teeth. I stopped momentarily and asked, "Why are you smiling?"

"Guess."

"Did it come?"

"Yes," she replied.

"Thank, God!" I said excitedly.

We smiled, said I love you to each other then proceeded to class. I danced and acted a fool the remainder of the day. Hearing the good news shocked me out of depression. Being back in rare form I couldn't wait to make love to her. All of a sudden I felt the spell on my balls being lifted. It had been almost three weeks and I was going bunkers worrying about not going to college, working like a dog, and being dead; it all seemed funny now. The dick was hard once again, but I allowed time for her cycle to run its course, another week's wait.

The following Saturday I was at her house. There was no one home but the two of us. This must be my lucky day, I thought. She put on some music and as usual we were very fluent when getting involved with each other. We didn't need any motivators to help us get started. Kissing was something we both enjoyed and it was always our starting point.

Once again we were located on the couch next to the bathroom since it was too risky to go upstairs. There was no escape route should someone come home during our love session, except going out of the second-floor window, and that was bolted shut. So as you can see the couch was our only option unless we went to a motel. The motel thing was definitely out of the question since neither of us had a job or any money.

With her underwear off and my pants pulled down to my ankles we positioned ourselves on the couch. We continued with foreplay then she allowed me to enter her. We found our rhythm while moving to the beat playing on the radio. I focused and stayed on her sensitive spot forcing her to cum much quicker than I would have if we had been in a more private location. Once again her eyes and movement were the key to my knowing when she was about to cum. Sensing this, I matched her stroke for stroke until we came together. Lying motionless on top of her while waiting for every drop of my cum to drain into her, I heard the key operating the lock to the back door. I ascended, pulled up my trousers in a rush and forgot my briefs, which were still down around my knees. After bringing Chinadoll back from la-la land I informed her that someone was entering the back door. She jumped up and ran to the bathroom that was nearby.

In a rush to zip my pants, I caught the skin around the head of my penis in the zipper. With no time to get it loose I sat down on the couch, grabbed a pillow and covered myself. In extreme pain from my ordeal, tears started to form in my eyes.

Returning from grocery shopping were her mother and grandmother. They entered the room I was in.

"Where is Chinadoll?" her mother asked.

"She's in the bathroom," I replied.

While walking back to the kitchen she turned and called my name, "Johnny!"

I was shaking like a tree in a wind storm. She asked me if her youngest son was home. I quickly answered, "No."

Once again, I was at the mercy of the Lord, and I was praying, "Lord, please don't let them ask me to help bring in the groceries, because you know the meat is hanging out of my pants, thawed, and dripping juice." I never would have been able to come back to that house again if my secret had been revealed.

At that moment I was so goddamn scared that I couldn't even feel the pain between my legs. When Chinadoll came out of the bathroom she looked lovingly at me. Pain must have been written all over my face because her disposition changed. I signaled to her, pointing down to my covered penis. She immediately went to the kitchen, greeted her mother and grandmother then started a conversation to allow me time to get to the bathroom.

I held both hands under my zipped-up cock in an attempt to catch the blood that was dripping at a steady rate. Once in the bathroom, biting hard on my shirt to keep from screaming, I undid the zipper, releasing my penis. Bleeding badly and in a lot of pain I wrapped myself in a wad of toilet paper. The top part of my trousers was soaked in blood so I washed them out in the sink as best as I could. To conceal my front, I pulled my shirt out of my pants and exited the bathroom. Chinadoll rushed over to me.

"What's wrong?"

"I caught my dick in the zipper and it's bleeding badly."

"Does it hurt?"

"Do I look like it hurt!"

"Yes."

"Okay! Check the pillow for blood."

"I will," she responded.

I told her I was leaving but would be back around eight o'clock.

"You all have a nice day," I said to her mother and grandmother and got the hell out of there.

Still in pain I went straight to my house. Trying to avoid my mother was virtually impossible since she was always watching and checking us to make sure that we didn't bring or wear anything home that she did not buy. This was part of her house security for preventing stealing. In other words, there was no reason to steal because we couldn't bring it home.

My mother observed right away that something was wrong. "What's wrong now?"

"Nothing."

"Boy, don't play with me."

"All right! I caught my penis in my zipper and it is hurting."

"Where did this happen?" she asked, while smirking.

"At Chinadoll's house."

She just laughed. I started thinking that maybe she knew exactly how it happened.

"Go and put something on it," she said between laughter.

Once in the bathroom I removed the wad of toilet paper and took a good, long soaking in the bathtub. By now the bleeding had stopped so I applied some peroxide then alcohol to aid with infection, and lastly, some Vaseline for a soothing effect.

Later that night, I went back to Chinadoll's house. I was thinking that it was a good thing her mother was not a Sherlock Holmes or a Dick Tracy like my mom, because if she was, I wouldn't have been there, I'd probably been dead. Chinadoll and I spent the rest of the evening talking and laughing about the big event of the day as well as all the other close calls we had had. Be as it may, we probably would have had sex on the porch that night if I wasn't zipped so badly.

CHAPTER 13

MOVING ON

Martin Luther King Jr. had been assasinated. It was a terrible tragedy and both Chinadoll and I were very sad, not to mention angry and hurt. We sat on her porch and watched all of the infuriated people flood the streets in a rage of violence, attacking anyone that was non-black. Fires erupted everywhere as stores owned by white merchants were torched one after the other. Stores that were not torched were broken into and looted, and all personnel of the white race were beaten without mercy.

I stayed with Chinadoll until about eleven that night then left for home. The streets were crowded with people of all ages. It was like being caught up in an earthquake or a volcanic eruption; everyone was scrambling trying to escape danger. In this case, the danger was the people themselves. I had no fear of what was going on because I knew most of the people and how to avoid trouble; also I was very aware of my limits. If I got in trouble it better be from something unavoidable because if the police didn't kill me my mother surely would. And God knows that I would rather face the police than the wrath of my mom. She was a very giving and caring person, but with her it was either black or white, no in between. You either did or you didn't and you paid dearly when what you did or didn't do didn't agree with her.

As I was walking home I ran into several close friends. They either expressed their views about King's death or tried to get me to participate in whatever actions they were involved in. All of us felt the loss of the man who had given hope to black Americans. We felt that our march to freedom had been slowed by the silent gunshot. We agreed that our dreams of becoming a free people was in disarray and wondered who would become the new drum major.

I realized that the majority of the people were out there just to be caught up with what was going on, while the minority was out for their own personal gain, looting. As the weeks went by things stayed much the same, the days were relatively calm, while the burning, looting and violence continued at night. Things were never the same in my community.

***

It was drawing close to the end of the school year and time for the senior prom. Chinadoll was not one for socializing when it came to large crowds so she didn't want to go to the prom. I knew how she felt because she'd refused to go to her own freshman class prom. However, she insisted that I go to the prom by myself. That was fine with me since I would rather stroll all night and dance with whomever I wanted to. So I went to the prom with one of my friends and had a fairly good time. Everyone knew that I was committed to the little freshman, as they called her, so they understood me showing up without a date. My dating Chinadoll didn't set too well with a few of the upperclass girls because they would have loved to ride the horse she was riding. But they knew, no chance.

The following day Chinadoll wanted to know all the details but there was very little to tell. Sensing that telling in small amounts caused suspicion, I decided to give a play by play of the night. I found it so amazing that the one person who didn't want to go to the prom sought after all the details. I was convinced she was making certain no one else rode her horse.

The first week of June 1968, graduation was approaching. Like most other schools we spent a lot of time preparing for the big day. I remember the teachers overseeing the commencement exercise and working us very hard as if we were training for the military. They wanted perfection on that day since our class was the largest graduating class ever at Gibbs Senior High School. Chinadoll was extremely excited for me and gave me a lot of encouragement as I prepared for my post high school years.

Finally, the big day came. Everyone was happy to have completed the first major milestone of their life, except those that were pulled from the line because they had failed to complete some of the requirements. Although that was quite embarrassing for those individuals, some of the teachers seemed to enjoy doing it. I guess that was their way of getting back at the unruly students.

Graduation day was especially gratifying for me since I had been told from early childhood that I would never amount to anything. Some people took my being outspoken and my readiness to defend myself as criminal. They based their conclusion on my attitude in the community rather than on my ability in the classroom. I had always been a good student, never having any problems competing academically. Also, it was a terrific day for my mother since I was the last of her six children, of which all had graduated from high school and one from college.

I showed up in the auditorium ahead of time for graduation. Chinadoll got there on time and sat with my mother. She was always a shy person who didn't say much, but my mother liked her a great deal. The graduation exercise went without any major flaws and all those in charge were happy. After graduation I took pictures, mostly with Chinadoll, a few with my mom and some with close friends. That night I went over to Chinadoll's house, and yes, you know what I wanted and got for my graduation present...pussy! You got it. Hot and juicy served with a whirlwind of booty rhythm. As always the night and my present were poetry full of ecstasy.

A couple of days following graduation, our class had a picnic day at Fort Desoto beach. As usual Chinadoll didn't want to go so I went alone with my friends Hickie and Zass. Hickie didn't have a special girlfriend at the time so he too went by himself; however, Zass's lady, Zill, was waiting for him at the beach party. We were about an hour late getting to the beach and Zass's girl was angry, to the point of being mad. We all got out of the car and walked down to the beach. Zill greeted her man then asked, "Where in the hell have you been?"

"I've been on my way out here," Zass responded. "Is there a problem?"

I knew from previous experience that all hell was about to break loose, so I positioned myself for a ringside seat. Zill continued to query Zass. Before he could explain and without warning, she hit him with a right jab that dropped him helpless. He was knocked-out momentarily. Everyone at the party was mumbling amongst themselves as to what took place; some louder than others, "Oh, shit! Did you see what Zill just did to Zass?"

Now Hickie and I were in a state of hilarity, falling out on the ground, rolling around, laughing our asses off. When Zass came to I said, "Man, I know you are not going to take that shit!" I was just pushing him to get another ass whipping. The two of them fought for a few minutes before we stopped them. I told Zass that he needed to quit her and find someone he could whip. One thing was for sure, they were the life of the party.

The fight must have continued that night because the next day when I went to Zass's house, he had two black eyes. I told him once again that a man didn't need a woman that could kick his ass—that was suicidal.

"Either you go to the gym and build some muscles or get a weak girlfriend like your ass," I said.

I never believed in hitting a woman, but I did feel the need to be in charge. I had never hit Chinadoll and exhibited no intentions of doing so, but then she wouldn't hit me. Further, unlike Zass I demonstrated that I could lead with good intentions, therefore earning the respect of my woman.

***

The first shock of graduating from high school was that I had to go to work and support myself. The summer jobs I had were simply to afford a new outfit or pay my way on dates. My mother had struggled all her life and there was no way she was going to allow me to live free. She couldn't afford to send me to college, much less pay for my expenses. With the help of one of the vice president's that my mother did day work for, I received a summer job at Honeywell Aerospace, Incorporated, in St. Petersburg, Florida. Considering some of the other jobs that my friends had, the salary wasn't bad. I had to get up early for work so I went to bed earlier than usual. That reduced the amount of time during the week that I spent with Chinadoll, but on the weekends we squeezed every second out of each minute of every day to express our love.

Early that summer, Chinadoll and her family went on a two-week vacation to Pennsylvania to visit her uncle. That was the loneliest and most miserable time I had ever experienced. I missed her tremendously and couldn't wait for her to get back home. Even though she called me each week it wasn't like being with me.

Upon her return I hurried over to her house and greeted her with lots of hugs and kisses; it was like tasting sugar for the first time. All of the family remained downstairs so we just talked and shared the events of the past two weeks. The longer I sat gazing into those gorgeous oriental-eyes, the hornier I became.

For some reason the rest of the family decided that they were going to stay downstairs all night. It appeared that they had come up with this master plan to sweat me out in an attempt to make my life miserable. Ordinarily, I could deal with that, but after not having any sex for two long weeks, my nuts were hard and aching. In plain simple terms that only meant one thing, I needed some loving. I was going to stick my dick somewhere that night, even if I had to bend it around and stick it up my own ass.

I looked at the clock. It reflected 10 p.m. and as you know my curfew was 11 p.m. Getting some pussy that night was worth getting an ass whipping for getting home late. I made up my mind that I was not leaving until the cock vomitted. So I came up with a plan of my own. I decided that Chinadoll and I would sit on the porch. I had noticed from previous occasions that there existed one dark corner on the porch, and tonight I owned it. Once out on the porch, I stood with my back to the wall and pulled Chinadoll close to me. I kissed her passionately on the lips and softly on the neck and earlobes until she became aroused.

Rotating her until her back was pressed against my chest; I continued to kiss her on her neck and eased my hand underneath her loosely fitted dress and into her panties, feeling the wetness of her excitement. Moving in front of her while unzipping my pants I pressed her back against the wall and raised her legs, spreading her cunt to accept my long, hard cock. She made a groaning noise as I pushed it deep inside her; as if this time I had too much meat for the bun. After two weeks, the usual thoroughbreds had turned into quarter horses and were cumming fast and hard.

Trying not to make too much noise proved difficult as we both missed the joy of lovemaking that had become a routine. Upon hearing our vocal expressions, her father called out to her. Still hard inside her and wanting more I lowered her legs and moved behind her, placing my dick back inside her as she opened the door, stuck her head inside and answered him, "Yes, Daddy!"

"It's late and time to come in," he instructed.

With me still inside her, moving very easy, she replied, "Okay, Dad, I'm cumming."

But what she should have said was, "Okay, Dad, Pookey's cumming," because I had just busted my nut for the second time. I slipped myself back into my pants and left on my short walk home.

I arrived home about 11:45 p.m. and could tell that my mom had an attitude, but before she could start in on me I said, "Sorry, Mom. Chinadoll just got back in town today and her parents let me stay a few minutes longer." The sorry Mom thing always worked. If I had gone in with an attitude to match hers I probably would have been knocked out for the night. Then the next day, I would have had to apologize and eat crow. So I just circumvented a potenially bad situation.

One day I was on my way to Harden's grocery store when I spotted Doria sitting in a car with her new boyfriend. I had heard that she was dating someone much older than her. The fact that he had a job and a car I was sure made him more attractive. Her son was also in the car; perhaps getting acquainted with his daddy-to-be. I was sure that she noticed me walking by but acted very nonchalant, pretending that she was not aware of my presence. I felt nothing emotionally; however, I still wondered at times whether or not her child was mine. All I could do was wish her well and hope that she found love and happiness as I did.

***

I still hadn't made up my mind as to where I would be going to college. Several schools were interested in me playing football, but I hadn't made a decision. Unfortunately, my school of choice had not shown any interest, so I waited until the last minute before deciding.

Miles College in Alabama had shown the most interest, offering me a full scholarship with all expenses paid. I was thinking, this is 1968 and black folks living in Alabama are afraid to live there, so why would anyone from Florida want to go to school there? Besides, the recruiter was a gay minister and that didn't set well with me. The thought of riding all the way to Alabama with him was not my idea of a good start in life.

Being honest with myself, I have to admit that Chinadoll was the real culprit in making my decision. The truth of the matter was I didn't want to go far away from home. I wanted to be close enough to come home a couple of weekends during the month. Most of my friends were afraid to go away for fear of losing their girl to someone else.

That was not my problem as I believed Chinadoll and I were forever. At least I knew that I was, even if she wasn't.

By late August I still hadn't made a decision about college, probably because the scholarship that I wanted didn't come through. Knowing that I had to act fast, I decided on calling the University of Tampa to see if they were interested in my playing for them. Upon making the call the coach requested that I come by the following day, Saturday. I paid a friend $10 to take me to Tampa; Hawkbeek came along for the ride.

When I arrived, the head coach and his scouting assistant were waiting to interview me. I presented them with clippings from the newspaper highlighting my plays during my senior season in high school. Fortunately for me the assistant coach had scouted me during one of my best games. I had caught eight passes that night. On his recommendation I was given a full scholarship. I was provided with practice gear and told practice was at 2 p.m.

"See you on the field," said the coach.

Knowing that the injury to my right side hadn't healed and I was not in football condition, I was determined to be the best that I could. At the beginning of practice I felt good, even though a little winded. I caught every pass during the warm-up drills. We were doing two on three blocking drills when one of the huge linemen hit me in the side with his knee; I felt pain equal to that of my original injury. I knew then and there that my football career had ended. I left that day, never to return.

Back in July I had sent an application to Florida A & M University but had not received any response. I remember feeling very confused during that time and didn't really know what steps to make. There was no male figure in my house to give me advice and my mother was not up on those things so I was lost. I was thinking how this was one time a father would have come in handy, as I wondered how many other brothers failed in life from lack of guidance.

Two weeks before I was to enroll at FAMU their letter of acceptance came in the mail. Previously, I had received a one-year academic scholarship from the pastor of a church whom my mother did day work for—my destiny was set.

Preparing to leave for college came with ease, but leaving Chinadoll became increasingly hard at the passing of each day. I didn't want to be without her. The night before I left we shared our love in every way imaginable. In addition to her being sad she was very worried that I would meet someone and forget about her. I assured her, in fact, guaranteed her that that could and would not ever happen. I hoped that made it crystal clear that my heart belonged to her. I had become tame and she possessed my soul. Possession of me was not something that she earned, it was a gift. That reward was given the first time I laid eyes on her.

The following day I took a Greyhound bus to Tallahassee, Florida to attend college at FAMU, also known as the Hill; a place that was foreign to me. I took a cab to Gibbs Hall, the dormitory where I was to live, accompanied by one footlocker—a 2-foot wide by 4-foot high chest with a lock in the middle and two more on the side. I remember getting out of the cab thinking that I didn't want to be there. I fought every second not to go back home. I knew that life for a black man, especially without an education, was unbearable so I asked myself, "Where are you going, back to the project?"

As much as I hated being at school I knew that I had to stay and succeed. How else could I provide a better life for my Chinadoll?

I was assigned a room that day in what was called the

Basement, since it was below ground level. My roommate was a senior, and a basketball player. He deserves most of the credit for my settling in and adjusting so well. He was a great guy with good habits. He spent a lot of his time enlightening me about what it took to survive on campus. He had checked in ahead of me and had set the room up. On display was his personal stereo system and lots of records, which he gave me permission to use. I thought that was a good beginning.

It had been almost a month since I had seen Chinadoll. I decided to go home one weekend to see my baby, I had missed her an awful lot. I caught a ride with a friend on a Friday after class; we arrived before dark that evening. I talked to my mother briefly about the first month of school then hurried to shower and dress. After dressing I scurried to Chinadoll's house. She was ecstatic to see me and greeted me with hugs and kisses. We talked and talked as we shared with each other all the happenings since we were last together. We were one bundle of joy. Her parents were glad to see me also. Her father allowed us to use the car to get pizza, but I also had an itch that needed scratching and I knew the perfect spot to accomplish it, my old reliable hideout that we had used so many times. After eating pizza we drove to our retreat. For the next hour we made love slowly, without haste, while enjoying each delicate second of our time together. That was our moment of truth. Once again we had affirmed our love. The rest of the weekend was quite joyous as we immersed ourselves in one another.

Back on the Hill I felt more relaxed. I guess it was because my emotions were still at peak level from the weekend.

One day my homeboys and I were hanging out on the set watching people, particularly the ladies as they walked by. Since being in school I had not seen anyone that was interesting to me. That was probably because of my commitment to Chinadoll. But, on this day while observing the view, my sight abruptly changed to admiration as a goddess passed within my visual spectrum. She was glamorous, wrapped in a smooth layer of elegance, unlike any other I had ever seen. I immediately queried my homies as to her identity. They quickly revealed that I didn't want to pursue her because she was untouchable.

Feeling confident I replied, "Everyone can be had by someone."

They just looked at me as if to say there goes another fool.

A few days later I just happened to be walking behind her. I increased my steps and caught up with her.

"Hello, my name is Johnny, would you mind if I walk with you?"

"My name is Wes, and no I don't mind you walking with me."

I continued walking with her. As we were passing the set to her dormitory, I noticed some of my homies watching as we went by. Wes and I talked for a few minutes outside then she went inside to study. As I was leaving I bumped into one of my homegirls who lived in the same dorm. I took the opportunity to make inquiries about Wes. She gave me a historical breakdown, where she was from, her age, who she was dating and other pertinent information. Also, she confirmed what my homeboys had said...this one would not be easy.

I had nothing to lose because my heart was in St. Petersburg, and I wasn't about to give her up. True love had a built-in security system that prevented me from straying by flashing a constant reminder (fear of losing) of my love supreme. I figured that I would enjoy the chase since no one else was willing.

Being aware of Wes's schedule I figured out when I would plan to meet her. When the time came I decided to dress to impress. I got up early that morning, took a shower, put on my only suit—a black Mohair wool with a light-blue shirt, black-and-blue silk tie, and alligator shoes. I was on it.

I intentionally arranged to be about five minutes late for my history class to demand full attention when I entered. There were a couple of attractive ladies in the class who might be worth the effort, so I figured I'd give them all something to dream about. A little pizzazz, I thought, would come in handy later on.

As planned, I strolled into the classroom and totally interrupted the session. My teacher, who was very gay, dramatically stopped me for all to see. At that moment, I thought my shit was the only shit that didn't stink. With everyone's eyes focused on me, Mr. Bufkin, hands on his hips in a gay man's pose said, "A $300 outfit on a 30-cent body." The whole class went berserk bringing the history period to an end, and boy, did my shit stink. I was totally humiliated, but refused to be degraded. I stood motionless for about ten minutes until the room became completely silent then asked, "But do you like what you see?"

Mr. Bufkin twisted his hips, smiled, and with no response, pranced his tight booty to the front of the class.

That afternoon as scheduled, I had a rendezvous with Wes and found her to be very jovial. With a delightful smile she said, "The outfit is definitely worth $300 and the body, at least $30. OK, obviously the teacher wasn't seeing what I'm seeing."

"All you see is $30?" I asked.

"I said at least $30. How much beyond that is for me to know," she chuckled.

Occasionally, over the next few weeks I would visit Wes in her dormitory. We would sit in the guest room and talk for hours discussing various issues. I had great respect for her and viewed her as someone worldly that I could learn from. Her vocabulary was superior to mine, which gave her somewhat of an advantage during conversation. I recall one discussion when we were debating an issue on relationships and she used the word extrapolate as she explained her point of view. I was totally lost. Therefore, I could no longer argue the issue.

I admired her style and appreciated her gracefulness. Those fine qualities were reflected by her unique character. She was the only woman I had known who took me completely out of my rhythm without any effort on her part. No matter how sophisticated my game plan was, it didn't work on Wes. Somehow I defeated myself without her ever having to say no, and I thought I was good! She was better than the player and didn't have a clue as to what she was doing. Her style definitely was not what I was used to. Over a period of time, Wes and I developed a platonic love, accepting each other unconditionally for who we were.

With the exception of studying, which I did very little, gambling consumed the majority of my free time. There was no need to chase girls since my heart was promised to Chinadoll, so playing cards for money was used to fill the void.

I hooked up with one of my homeboys named Smackie, who was a senior and biology major. We grew up in the same neighborhood and our families still remained close. Smackie was married with two children. He taught me a lot about gambling, especially how to cheat at cards.

We would stay up late at night to mark the cards by removing the cellophane with a hair dryer, then the stamp. After the cards were marked, they were placed back in the box, and glue was put on the stamp and the plastic to reseal. That was foolproof. The next day when the game was about to start we would throw a new deck on the table. No one had any suspicions as to how they were robbed. I had more money than people with jobs.

I remember one weekend in particular when Smackie had a card party at his apartment. The game was open to anyone wanting to play. It started Friday and continued through Sunday. There were several ladies at the party preparing food, drinks and anything else that would ensure a lively gathering.

By Saturday night almost everyone was broke with the exception of Smackie, his roommate (O.T.), his neighbor, and yours truly. We interrupted play Saturday night about 11 p.m. to sleep, with the understanding that the game would continue at 10 a.m. Sunday.

Two hours after the game resumed, only three players were left as Smackie's neighbor tapped out. About this time O.T.'s girlfriend asked him to go to the store for a bell pepper. Since he was on a winning streak, he told her he was not going to the store for no damn bell pepper. Now, the rest of us felt that his attitude was less than reasonable because the ladies were preparing food for all of us. So we insisted that he go since he was the one who requested the meatloaf in the first place, but old O.T. said no with an attitude.

Not wanting to deal with him being obnoxious, his girlfriend made the meatloaf without the peppers. The smell of the food teased us until it was time to eat.

Being roommates with Smackie, O.T. was aware of his card wizardry so he decided not to play against him in less than a four-man game. That meant that he would have to play me head up, and that wasn't good for him because I was better.

Approximately two hours later good old O.T. was dead broke. He had lost $250 in cash and owed another $200 in IOU's. Everyone could tell that he wanted to cry as his eyes brewed and he pouted like a two-year-old kid who had just gotten a spanking. After a few seconds of observing his face we all burst into laughter. He then started boo-hoo crying and said, "I knew I should have gone for that bell pepper. If I had I might still have some money."

"Don't worry, honey. At least the meatloaf was good," his girlfriend said with a smirk.

The following Sunday I hosted a three-man card game that included Smackie, Big Joe, who was a really mean football player standing at 6'10" and weighing 290 pounds, and of course me. Big Joe had just received his war check from the government for educational expenses.

From the beginning, Smackie and I had our marked deck in the game. I started off winning and had won about $80 of Big Joe's money. All of a sudden he stopped the game and said, "I know you motherfuckers are cheating. I have never seen niggas read cards as good as ya'll."

At that time, Smackie and I were scared shitless. There was no way for us to escape because Big Joe was between us and the door. So we just played it cool and prayed silently. I was looking around the room for a weapon just in case he found the markings on the cards. After scrutinizing the cards for what seemed like a lifetime, he made mention that he couldn't find any scratches. Both Smackie and I breathed a sigh of relief. Big Joe would have never found any scratches because we used ink the color of the cards to mark them. He was looking for the wrong thing. Thank the Lord!

When things finally settled, Big Joe decided he wanted to play one of us at poker. Since Smackie was better at poker, I decided to let him play; furthermore, I was $80 ahead and scared, so quitting while at the forefront seemed to be the most logical thing to do.

Since I had an early class the following morning I decided to turn in. Around 1 a.m. Smackie woke me up, asking to borrow $40, which I gave him then went back to sleep. Again, around 3 a.m., I was awakened to the request of another $40 which I kindly gave, but made it crystal clear to Smackie that I didn't want any shit when it came time to collect my money. This was to defray any thoughts Big Joe might have had. I thought, as I dosed off to sleep, that Smackie was in deep trouble, but I didn't let it bother me because I had already won and he was indebted to me....and he would pay.

At 7 a.m. I was awakened to sounds of Smackie shouting, "I have trimmed the duck and busted his ass." I got up and joined him, jumping and shouting in jubilation when an unexpected knock was heard at the door.

"Who is it?" I asked.

"It's me, Big Joe," he replied in a deep thunderous voice.

At that moment Smackie looked like he was about to shit in his pants.

"Oh, shit! Do you think he heard us?" asked Smackie.

"Heard us?" I whispered. "I didn't say anything. But I tell you what, I'm going to hit that big motherfucker with this chair and we're going to get the fuck out of here."

Smackie opened the door and to our relief our rejoicing had gone unheard.

In his deep, thunderous voice Big Joe said, "Hey man, I don't like no one bothering me, so I don't want you niggas to tell anyone what happened because I don't want to have to kill none of you motherfuckers."

We quickly assured him that he didn't have to worry about us telling anyone because we didn't want to be dead. Big Joe left and that was the last time I played cards against him.

CHAPTER 14

GETTING SCREWED

The weekend before Thanksgiving a group of the guys decided to go to the Classic in Daytona Beach. Smackie, two of his roommates Tom and Will, and two ladies went on the trip. They rented one room with two beds where all five of them stayed. O.T. couldn't go because I'd left him broke a couple weeks before.

Will was in love with one of the ladies, Gertha, and was spending a lot of money in pursuit of her. She had no interest at all in him but since Will worked and was the only one who had money, he became a part of her master plan. He was an easy trick because the others all knew that he would flash money and showboat in the presence of the lady he thought was his. The real deal was that Smackie was fucking her and had been for some time; all at Will's expense. Will would buy the food and the wine, Smackie would drink the wine, eat the food and the pussy. Will was getting fucked every which way but loose. Get the picture.

That night at the motel Will wanted his lady to sleep with him in one of the beds since he had paid for the whole trip. Gertha made it known to Will that she had no intentions of sleeping with him then indicated that she was going to sleep with Smackie. Will got pissed off and went off into a frenzy.

"I'll be goddamn if I'm going to foot the fucking bill and my woman sleep in the bed with another fucking nigga," he yelled.

Smackie was so scared to open his mouth as he knew Will would put his ass out in the street if he became aware of him banging his woman, so he kept his mouth shut.

Gertha then indicated that she had a bright idea for the sleeping arrangements. She decided that Smackie, Will and herself would sleep in the same bed. That arrangement made sense to Will since there were only two beds and Tom and his lady had the other one. However, during the course of the night Will, who had been drinking, fell asleep so his girlfriend placed Smackie in the middle and she got in bed on the other side. With Will out cold, snoring and farting from the baked beans he had eaten earlier, Smackie and Gertha fucked the night away.

Ironically, Will spent all his money sponsoring the trip and was the only one who didn't get fucked. He was also the only one who got fucked, sad.

The Wednesday before Thanksgiving 1968, everyone was preparing to go home for the break. Will had decided that he would drive home accompanied by Gertha. For some reason the boy refused to see things as they were. That lady had no interest at all in him. He had never kissed her much less had sex with her, so one had to wonder where he was getting his vibes from, perhaps from a wet dream.

Anyway, hoping that he would have gotten the message after the Daytona trip and trying not to hurt his feelings she told him that she was driving her own car and that Smackie was going along to assist with the driving. Will asked Smackie if that was true, and he said yes. Smackie then stated that I would ride with Will to keep him company. If the truth be told, I was Smackie's cover.

Off on our journey we went with Smackie following Will. About one hour into our trip Will asked, "Do you think Gertha is sitting too close to Smackie?"

Now as you know, I was Smackie's best friend and there was no way I was going to help Will in any way.

"I can't tell because they are too far back," I replied, knowing all the time the game plan and what was going on. Then Mister Intelligent decided that he was going to slow down and see for himself. Seeing that Will had slowed down, Gertha moved over, killing whatever suspicions Will had.

After Smackie pulled ahead approximately one-half mile I could tell that Gertha had moved once again closer to him but my lips were sealed.

Shortly thereafter Will shouted, "Pookey, don't it look like she has moved closer to him? Her head is under the rearview mirror."

"Man, it's so foggy I can't see clearly," I replied. "Besides, I'm nearsighted."

He went ballyhoo and said, "Motherfucker you know what's going on. You are Smackie's main man and anything he does, you know and right now you are covering for his ass."

"I don't know what's going on and if something is going on it's none of my fucking business. You live with him, you should know him better than anyone," I shouted back.

"Motherfucker I ought to put your ass out of my car right here in these woods and let them peckerwoods kick your ass," he shouted.

"Bitch, you ain't putting me out a motherfucking thing. If you got a problem take it up with Smackie," I yelled.

Will got belligerent driving at speeds of up to 80-miles-per-hour. We were riding in a Toyota Corona and it felt like it was coming apart at the seams. The car was not built for that type of speed. I was nervous because that fool was mad enough to kill everybody.

Finally, he caught up to Smackie who had slowed down as he approached the town of Chiefland. Will signaled for him to pull into the truck stop. I knew that wasn't going to work because Smackie always had some shit up his sleeve. Dumb ass Will was dumber than dumb and was inferior to Smackie's way of thinking.

I kept my mouth closed for fear that the idiot would crash into another car, killing us all. Smackie nodded in acknowledgment as Will went by. Will pulled into the truck stop more wired than a lit stick of dynamite. I had observed Smackie's failure to follow directions, but Will was unaware that when he turned off the main highway, Smackie kept going. Will got out of the car, waiting for Smackie to show up, but to his surprise that never happened. I acted as if I was just as confused as he was in order to keep his anger under control with me. We waited for about fifteen minutes then Will said, "I'm going to catch them motherfuckers and kick both of their asses!"

I still can't figure out why he waited so long when they were right behind us. Do the math.

Back in the car we headed for the highway. I reminded Will that we were low on gas.

"To hell with gas. I have to catch them before they get too far," he bellowed.

Off we went again at 80-miles-per-hour in a goddamn Corona, which as I said felt as if it was about to fall apart, trying to catch a 3-speed Mustang with a high performance engine. I was so angry with Smackie for putting me in that situation that if we did catch him I was going to help Will kick his ass.

We had been driving at a speed of more than 80 for an hour, and still the other car was not in sight. Knowing Smackie, his driving speed was about 90-miles-per-hour, which meant that he had more than increased his distance between us. I made every attempt to share this theory with my traveling companion but he refused to listen to reason, in fact, he wouldn't listen to God at that time.

Once again, I reminded him that the car was just about out of gas. He insisted that we only had one hour driving time left and could make it home. He further stated that he had driven that distance without fueling on many occasions.

"Yes, maybe so. But your fat, cheap ass was driving 55-miles-per-hour, burning less gas," I said.

About fifteen minutes later the car started sputtering and loss power. "God I hope nothing is wrong with the engine," Will whispered.

I was so mad. Mad enough to hurt that dumb son-of-a-bitch. "You damn skippy something is wrong with the engine. It doesn't have any gas to give it power, you stupid bastard. Now I'm stuck out here in these dark-ass woods with your dumb ass," I yelled.

"Fuck you," he shouted. That was his favorite phrase.

Now I was fuming. "Fuck me. You mean fuck you! You damn right Smackie is fucking your woman! He's been fucking her the whole semester and you have been paying for his pleasure. He fucked her in Daytona Beach the night you got drunk and fell asleep. If you didn't know it then, you didn't want to know, so it's your own damn fault. Don't fuck with me anymore tonight because you have caused me not to see Chinadoll and I'm mad as a motherfucker," I shouted.

After we finished arguing I lay back in my seat, locked the door, and got as comfortable as I could under the circumstances. There was no way I was going to walk in the pitch black dark of the night in peckerwood country. Hell no!

Observing Will staring at me I said, "Don't even look at me because it's your fault so get your chubby ass to jogging." He was more afraid of the dark than I was. Knowing that, I decided to play with him by scaring him further. Acting as if I was dosing I made noises by scratching and lightly tapping with my hand that was next to the door. I could feel him jumping as he looked around in the direction the noise was coming from.

Unwilling to reveal myself I laughed internally. For the first time during that trip I was having fun. Hearing more noises he shook me and asked me if I heard something. Appearing dazed I replied, "Heard what?" Then suggested that he go outside and see.

Admitting fear he said, "I'm scared, you come go with me." I informed him that I was trying to sleep and for him not to bother me anymore.

Unable to hold my laughter any longer I made a loud noise as if someone was trying to enter the door, then I screamed loudly and grabbed his arm. He returned my scream, knocked my hand away then opened the door and ran down the road screaming and hollering like the crazy fool he was, that made my night and missing my baby worthwhile.

A few minutes later he came back accompanied by the highway patrol. There was a gas station about one-half mile up the road just around the curve. The officer put in just enough gas for us to get to the gas station. Feeling jolly, I decided to be a bit sarcastic. "Do you still think you can catch them?" I said smiling. He gave no response, not even his favorite fuck you. I laughed myself to tears never telling him that I was the culprit making the noise.

After losing about two and a half hours on the highway, I arrived safely home at approximately 10 p.m. As

I opened the car door I thanked Will for the ride. Knowing he was mad as hell I said, "Here's wishing you and your wife a most pleasant and loving holiday."

He looked at me angrily and shouted, "Fuck you and the holiday too."

It was much too late for me to go to Chinadoll's house so I called her and gave her all the details of the evening. We laughed and talked until sleep took possession of our bodies.

The next morning I walked across the field to Smackie's house and gave him play-by-play details of last night.

Chinadoll had invited, as well as insisted, that I have Thanksgiving dinner with her family. Feeling more comfortable with them I accepted. Dinner was great; however, I didn't pig out like I would have if I had been at home. The Saturday night that followed, we decided to go out for pizza as we were truly tired of turkey. Our private little spot was still there and yes, our love was solemn as our warm bodies welded together. Chinadoll and I had once again bonded, pledging our love to one another.

As I departed that Sunday afternoon I was left with the feeling that a lifetime of loving her would still be too short. Smackie decided to drive his car back to school so I rode with him. Besides, there was no way I was going to ride with that other idiot; I had opened a Pandora's box. Smackie was relieved that the truth was out in the open. Once back on campus, Smackie and Will worked out all of their problems.

The first session of my college life had come to a close. I did fairly well with the exception of the "D" that I received for English composition. I wasn't too upset as I knew from the start that writing compositions was not my forté. I was a mathematics major and would rather solve 100 problems than read one chapter. College was not what I wanted to do, but what I needed to do, and I was determined to overcome any and all obstacles because in a couple of years I would have a wife and children to support. Chinadoll was proud of me having successfully completed my first term in college.

CHAPTER 15

TRICK OR TREAT

Christmastime was very exciting as usual. It was my time to spend with my lady of choice, enjoying her to the fullest during my stint home. We cherished each minute we spent with one another, never missing out on an opportunity to nourish our sexual appetite.

The New Year seemed to have come and gone in a haste. I was scheduled to ride back to school with Smackie, but to my surprise, he informed me that he wasn't going back to college. His decision did not make sense, as he only had two semesters left before completing his degree in biology. I asked him if he was nuts, while trying to get him to see that this was not the right thing to do. He didn't give me much detail supporting his decision but I assumed that it had to do with infidelity. Yes, married Smackie who was having an affair with Gertha, had just found out that his wife was cheating on him. Even so, I tried to get him to realize that finishing school was necessary in order to guarantee a quality life. "Besides, you have come too far to quit now," I told him. He refused to be logical and would not listen to reasoning so I wished him good luck and went on my way.

How could a person be as academically inclined as he was, and be so unintelligent about the basic principles of survival? I thought as I walked away.

I elected to spend what was left of the day with Chinadoll and caught the 11 p.m. bus back to Tallahassee, arriving about 7 a.m. Monday.

On Thursday morning at about 7:30, Smackie showed up at my door. He indicated to me his plans once again, to quit college and move to New Jersey. He told me that he had found out that his wife was cheating on him, and that he had overheard a telephone conversation between her and the boyfriend. My family and I were very aware of his wife's unfaithfulness since we had observed her with the boyfriend late at night slipping into her boyfriend's cousin's house, which was located behind us. As this was none of our business we kept our lips sealed, as I did in his case.

As the saying goes, "What's good for the goose is good for the gander." For some reason, men think that it's all right for them to cheat, and when they are busted, they expect to be forgiven. But when the shoe is on the other foot, they are ready to put their wife's or girlfriend's head under a guillotine.

In my case I was not cheating on Chinadoll and didn't expect her to cheat on me. I reminded him that he too had been disloyal then suggested that they try harder to work it out, if not for them, for the two kids. He said that his mind was made up and that he was leaving on the 11 p.m. bus. He then indicated that he had one problem, he was broke.

"How in the hell are you going to New Jersey with no money?" I asked, a little frustrated with his stupidity.

"I have a friend there who will be helping me once I arrive."

"How much do you need?"

"The ticket is $38.95," he replied.

I gave him $40 and sadly told him to take good care of himself. The evening following that day he was supposed to leave, but he showed up again at my room. I asked him what was going on and he told me that he had spent the night with Gertha and had wined and dined on the money I had given him. He wanted to know if I could lend him another $40.

"Do I look like fucking Will? Now you want me to pay for your pussy?" I shouted at him.

With his head down looking like a basset hound, he said, "I'm sorry, I'll pay you back."

"No problem, I said. But this time I'm going to the bus station and purchase the ticket."

That night I bought the ticket, put him on the bus, and gave him the change from the $40 for food. "Spend this $1.05 wisely because you have a long ride ahead," I said.

**

My birthday had come around again and that year I was nineteen years old. I had just received a letter from my sweetheart, saying how much she loved me and wished me a happy birthday. That night, I called and thanked her for the beautiful and comforting words. It was those little things that made my being away from her more tolerable. During our conversation, she told me that she had written lyrics from a song to me in her history book. She began to sing as I listened:

Every morning when I wake up
you know I sit right down and I say to myself
Girl, don't you know you'd be so blue
if the boy you been loving ever up and left

You got legs so you can walk
the man gave you a voice so that you can talk
If you love the man I think you really ought
to tell him, before he gives his loving to
some other woman

So I say I dig you, Pookey, tell the world I do
I really love you Baby, yes I do.

Sign, your wife (with love)

Then she wrote: To my husband on his birthday, a kiss from me. Do well in school, Pook! Dated February 1, 1969.

Days after receiving Chinadoll's letter, my need to see her became intense. Spring break was about six weeks away, which was too long to bear, but I had no choice because classes were difficult and studying on the weekends was necessary.

At last, spring break arrived and I was on my way home to see my baby. While at home my brother stopped by and informed everyone that he had found the girl of his dreams and planned to get married. The wedding was scheduled to take place in August with the vows being exchanged in her hometown, Detroit.

Finally, some lucky woman had conquered the town's most eligible bachelor. She was good-looking, educated and came from a well-to-do family. She also happened to be the daughter of one of Detroit's most well-known bishops. I would say that those were the qualifications required to tame the Buddy as he was affectionately called. Everyone in the family was quite excited that our playboy had decided to settle down. I was hoping that his woman would be mean-spirited with broad shoulders and a tough hide because some of my sisters could be brutal. I don't think any of them, especially my eldest sister, felt there was anyone good enough for him. As for me, I was happy if he was happy. I didn't have to live with her.

Before I knew it it was summer, and as usual it was hot and sticky. My first year in college was very successful as I produced a good grade point average. Fortunately for me I was able to get my summer job back with Honeywell. That allowed me to save the money necessary to return to school in the fall. Also, it allowed Chinadoll and I to indulge in various forms of entertainment over the summer. The majority of my time outside of work was spent with Chinadoll, doing whatever it took to replenish the love jug and ensure her that the time she spent alone while I was away at school did not go unappreciated. I often expressed how fortunate and how blessed I was to have her in my life. God had been good to me.

We had the whole house to ourselves one day, and we made good use of it. Making love to her was always good and exciting. We never held anything back, always opening our souls. Someone once asked the question, what goes up and never comes down? I could truly answer that with four simple words, "My love for Chinadoll."

After we finished making love, we sat as we often did, talking and singing our favorite songs. The song most dearest to our hearts was written by Marvin Gaye, performed as a duet with Tammie Terrell. Gazing into each others eyes we would sing the first two verses of *If This World Were Mine*.

My verse

If this world were mine, I would place at your feet
all that I own, you been so good to me
If this world were mine I'd give you the flowers the
*   birds*
*   and the bees*
And with your love beside me that would be all I need
If this world were mine I'd give you anything

Chinadoll's verse
If this world were mine, I would make you a king
with wealth untold you could have anything
If this world were mine I give you each day so sunny
and blue
And if you wanted the moonlight I'd give you that too
If this world were mine, oh Baby, I'd give you
anything…

CHAPTER 16

TAKING A CHANCE

My family and I flew out of Tampa one day en route to Detroit for my brother's big day. That day was special and sacred like it should have been. That would be the beginning of the end for his dick, which no longer would be free to roam in the drawers of all those women. The playboy had played his last game.

Chinadoll was sad, but supportive about my having to leave. My trip was to last two weeks. After the wedding activities in Detroit my brother had arranged for everyone to fly to New York for a second reception. Afterwards, I would spend the remaining time with my sisters who lived there.

We arrived on time and were driven to the rehearsal party by a member of the bride's family. My sisters and their husbands were already there as they had flown in from New York earlier that day. I couldn't help but notice the gorgeous girls, especially those of the wedding party. But as always, thoughts of Chinadoll filled my space.

Shortly after arriving, my brother informed me that one of the groomsmen was unable to participate; he asked if I would be his replacement. Of course I said yes.

The wedding went on as planned and was more beautiful than any I'd attended. I couldn't help but notice the groom's nervousness as he stumbled and almost fell. I was just waiting for the playboy to faint so I could crack up, but he held his composure.

After the ceremony there was a grand reception with food and drink galore. We couldn't stay long because we had a 5 p.m. flight to catch.

The weather was terrible, lightning was extremely bad and we experienced tons of turbulence. Halfway to our destination lightning hit the plane, damaging the radar. At one point everyone, including the pilot, thought the plane was going to crash as we dropped a few thousand feet. There were some nuns accompanying us and they were all praying nonstop. I looked back at one of them and asked sarcastically, "How is your faith?" She cursed me out with her expression.

"God, if you want me, take me out of the plane now while I'm close to you. Whatever you do, don't let me go down to the ground, it will just be a waste of time," I prayed.

The pilot eventually stabilized the plane and all seemed well, with the exception that we were unable to land in New York. The radar was dead, making it impossible to guide us to a safe landing; therefore, we had to land in Newark, New Jersey. By the time we landed it was after 8 p.m., which was the starting time for the reception. After renting several cabs we were driven to the reception, arriving about 11 p.m. To our surprise, more than two thousand people had remained awaiting our arrival. Happy to have reached our destination alive, we ate and partied until the early morning hours.

The next day we went to Mama Leone's, a famous Italian restaurant, for Sunday dinner. For the first time in my life I had a seven-course meal. I had become used to the one-course meal I had several times a week consisting of pork 'n beans and wieners.

Already missing my baby, I decided to go home after spending less than one week in New York. Upon arriving home, I immediately went to Chinadoll's house where I spent the entire evening until curfew. The next day she came over to my house as planned since everyone else remained in New York. For the first time I had her all alone in my domain to do as I chose without fear of being discovered. Ordinarily, she would have been a bit nervous, but knowing that my family was away she was very relaxed. We lay in the bed with our clothes on talking about the time apart from each other. Talking soon changed to touching, which immediately shifted to heavy foreplay. Before long we were undressing each other, admiring our nakedness as if for the first time. While lying on her back, I kissed her entire body softly, being careful not to touch her most sensitive treasure. Her enticing body language prompted me to give her more, causing her to savor in ecstasy. I planted her reward deep inside her sending her into an orgasmic frenzy. She sweated profusely while screaming from deep within her soul.

"Oh, my God! What the fuck is happening to me?" she asked, as I continued to ram dick to her delight. The world stood still as the sound of her voice was carried throughout the neighborhood.

I was still fucking and she was still cumming so I kissed her passionately, taking her entire tongue into my mouth. The sensation felt from kissing her caused my cock to swell even larger, as if that was possible. Sensing that I was about to cum, she matched my rhythm. I came with the force of a volcano, throbbing, sending impulses throughout her body, leaving her immobile. Her expression was as calm as still waters, as her mind sank deep into the abyss of an unknown sexual voyage never before experienced. She lay tranquil with her eyes closed, caught between two worlds, the earthly one and the one I had just sent her to. I was thinking, no drugs and no gimmicks were used to send her to Pluto, just my desire and determination to please.

As we departed from my house I couldn't help but notice the neighbors staring us down with speculations of our involvement. We were unaffected by their stares because we had just reached a new level of awareness during our sexual ritual. However, I wondered how long it would take for my mother to hear about our being locked up for the day.

Chinadoll and I agreed to rendezvous at my house the following Saturday. My mother was scheduled to arrive home that evening so I decided to spend the hours between 1 and 5 p.m. with Chinadoll. That would allow time for us to get cleaned up before my mother's arrival. As always Chinadoll showed up right on time.

We didn't waste any time getting intimate, and before long we were locked together in each other's arms. The temperature was exceptionally hot and very humid, which contributed to our bodies being drenched with perspiration. We were draped in the cocoon of each other's passion as I moved on her with long, deep strokes.

Our lovemaking was so intense that we failed to hear the front door open. It was my mother returning. As she started up the stairs I heard her calling out to me asking if I was there. Jumping up I quickly closed my bedroom door, which couldn't lock.

"Yes, Mama I'm here. I'll be out in just a minute," I responded.

Chinadoll was a nervous wreck about to break like new china. We dressed quickly as I made every effort to calm her.

"When I open the door, I'll go into my mother's room and you slip downstairs," I said.

The instant I opened the door the smell of sex rushed out ahead of me straight into my mom's room. She met me as I entered her room.

"What the hell is that funky smell coming from your room?" she asked. "You need to go wash your ass because you smell like you haven't bathed since you've been back."

"I've been taking baths, Mama."

At that time she heard footsteps going downstairs. "Who is that going downstairs?"

"It's Chinadoll."

"What have ya'll been doing locked in your room?"

"Just talking and fooling around."

"Just talking my ass! You did more than talking to be smelling like that. And oh! You've been bathing alright, right between Chinadoll's legs. Both of you need to go wash your asses to get rid of that funk. You know that I'm not taking care of any babies and you can't afford to, so you best be careful."

"I'm careful, Ma!"

I begged her not to say anything to Chinadoll as I went to take a shower.

While walking Chinadoll home I noticed she was quiet. She was actually upset about the whole incident and was worried about how my mother felt about her. I assured her that she liked her a lot and everything was fine.

"My mother's bark is worse than her bite," I said. With my arms around her, we kissed as she quickly returned to her old self.

I hoped no one was at her house because as my mother said, she needed to go wash her ass. My baby's funk was reeking. Her parents would be able to smell her coming down the road, I thought.

"Baby, if anyone asks about that smelly odor just tell them that you were playing football with me in the project. Good, God Almighty!" I said, while making a "you stink" expression.

She chortled at the look on my face and said, "Boy, you crazy!"

When we arrived at her house her brother was in the living room watching television and her mother was in the kitchen preparing dinner. To ease the pressure, I immediately said to him, "Boy, you should have seen your sister playing football; she is almost as good as I am."

Like a fool, she tried to get in on the conversation, but I reminded her that she was stinking and needed to go upstairs and get a bath before someone started asking questions. Understanding the point, she hurried to the bathroom. Once again a close call; but a chance worth taking.

CHAPTER 17

UNHAPPY FEELINGS

Once again summer was over and I soon would be embarking to matriculate my sophomore year of college. As always, Chinadoll was saddened by the fact that I had to leave for school. I had known for some time that she got extremely lonely when I was away, and to make matters worse, one of her friends who had never had a boyfriend was jealous of our relationship and had been making attempts to feed her bad advice. I called her friend Miss Celie and if you are familiar with the movie *Color Purple*, then you know how she looked—a country, homely look, with an ugly face, nappy hair and a duck-like walk. Even knowing Miss Celie's intentions, I tried to be cordial when in her presence.

Besides, Chinadoll had insisted that she wasn't swayed by her friend's remarks and assured me that she had everything under control.

Getting back on campus was satisfying after a much successful freshman year. I no longer lived in the dormitory and felt that the privacy would help increase my GPA. I took over Smackie's room, which was an easy transition since I was familiar with his roommates. Each of them was much older than me, disciplined, and determined to graduate. That motivated me to do more studying.

The fall semester was the most pleasurable time of the year to be at FAMU. It was football season and people, old and young, were coming from all around to see the football game, especially, the halftime show featuring

America's #1 band, the Mighty Marching 100. There were parties all over the city and the ladies were out strutting their stuff as if on display waiting to be plucked.

On the first game day of the season I caught the eye of a beautiful art; she was pure poetry. I finally came to understand how David felt when he first laid eyes on Basheeba. I bopped right over to introduce myself.

"Excuse me, do you have a minute?"

"Sure."

"I'm Johnny."

"I'm Peaches."

"Of all the ladies I've seen today, you are by far the most beautiful."

"You think so?"

"I know so. Are you a freshman?"

"Yes, does it show?"

"Not really. It's just that I haven't seen you around before."

"Okay."

"Where are you from?"

"Georgia."

"I know you have to catch up with your friends but I'd like to see you again, just to talk."

"When?"

"Tomorrow."

"I'll be at the pool between one and four o'clock."

"I'll be there. Stay sweet!"

"I'll try."

When I arrived at the pool the next day she was already there wearing a bikini that fit as if it was painted on her body. As I stood admiring her beauty, my dick went into cardiac arrest from the massive blood rush being pumped from my heart to my loins. There was no way I could walk out on the pool deck with my cock bulging from my swimsuit.

Until that moment, I had thought Caramel was the finest thing on the face of the earth, but that girl in her bikini disrupted my entire nervous system. It took me about fifteen minutes of deprogramming before I could emerge to face her. As I greeted her, she touched me lightly across the chest and I completely lost it. My dick started rising at a rapid rate, coughing, as the juices of excitement started to flow. Reaching the fullness of erection, the head of my dick started to throb as it tried to expand beyond its bound. I removed the towel from my shoulders and tied it loosely around my waist in an attempt to hide the big dog in my swimsuit. She glanced down to admire the sudden growth, smiling while nodding expressions of appreciation.

"Is it me or some other bikini?" she asked.

"Is there anyone else here?" I asked. "Baby you have reached the core of my soul as the view is breathtaking," I said, as my expression reflected complete adoration.

That night, we went down to the patch, the band's practice field, to talk while watching the band members do their thing.

We communicated quite easily and enjoyed each other's company. The time seemed to fly by so fast. Curfew for girls was 11 p.m. so I walked her to her dorm. That was the first time since attending college that I had been so overwhelmed.

A couple of days later we sat talking in front of her dorm. She appeared to be distressed so I asked her if something was wrong. I assured her that I was willing to help in any way possible. She insisted that there was nothing I could do to remedy her problem. She then informed me that she would be leaving school tomorrow for good because her financial aid was disapproved. I was distraught. I was thinking, she's gone before I really got to know her. I was deeply saddened upon hearing of her dilemma as I felt that we would have become best of friends.

The truth of the matter was that I wanted to fuck her worse than a whore needing a trick. Chinadoll was still untouchable, but that time I sure would have indulged in a little college fun to get the kinks out of my dick.

As the moonlight reflected in her eyes I couldn't help but notice the tears dripping from her cheeks.

"I'm hurting not only because I don't have the money to stay in school, but because I won't have the opportunity to share what I feel with you," she said.

While kissing, we held each other tightly before saying our last good-bye. That night at curfew, I left in the shadow of her love, never to see her again. The following day after class I went to her dorm to find that she had vanished from my life as quickly as she had appeared.

A month had passed since I had last seen Chinadoll and as always I missed her deeply. Even in the midst of feelings blooming from Peaches's bud, I still cherished my sweet lady's love. Being in a college atmosphere with all of its temptations could cause me to stray, but I would come home to roost as Chinadoll was my true soul mate.

The Rattlers had an away game that week so I decided to go home for the weekend. My homegirl Manda asked me to ride home with her to assist with the driving. She was a good friend of my sister's and was a side thing for my brother during desperate times. She was the lady in his car the day he let me use his apartment to make love to Chinadoll. Her body was out of this world but that face, yuck! Anyway, she was very nice and as sweet as could be. We decided to leave at 4 p.m. so that we could reach home before it got too late. She drove an older Chevrolet that appeared to be in good condition, as I had driven home with her on several occasions. About two hours into our trip I smelled an odor, as if something was burning. Before long we could see smoke coming from under the hood. I stopped the car, raised the hood and saw that the electrical wires were on fire. Understanding the seriousness of the problem I told Manda to be prepared for a long night. Both her boyfriend and Chinadoll were expecting us at a pre-determined time, which was about 9 p.m. for my baby.

The fire appeared to have burned itself out after a short while but it rendered the car immobile. The night air was chilly but we refrained from sitting inside until I was sure the sparks wouldn't re-occur.

I was very familiar with the area of our breakdown since I had traveled the road many times before. We were located in a desolate stretch, miles outside of the city of Inverness, which was in the heart of Florida, dixie-pure redneck country. We had no gun for protection and nowhere to run except in the woods with the snakes and other wildlife. Once again, I was at the mercy of the Lord.

The sun had gone down and the temperature had dropped to the low 50s. There were no cars on the highway, probably because no one traveled that road except the highway patrol and us fools. When I broke down with Will I wasn't afraid because I knew he had a gun. But this time I was nervous. We sat in the car behind locked doors and waited for what seemed like forever.

It was so dark we had a hard time seeing each other. Finally, after several hours a highway patrol stopped to investigate the parked car. I told Manda to put both hands on the dashboard in plain view, and likewise, I put both of mine on the steering wheel. As the officer approached the car I could see from the side mirror that he had his gun drawn. I was thinking, I sure hope this is not one of those assassin cops trying to rid the world of niggers. Out there in those woods, he could have killed us and disposed of our bodies such that we would never have been seen or heard from again. Of course, if we were dead it wouldn't make a difference to us anyway.

To our surprise, the officer was very helpful after he heard of our dilemma. He drove us about 20 miles to the nearest truck stop. Manda placed a collect call to her boyfriend asking him to come and get us. He arrived approximately an hour and a half after the call.

By now the time was approaching 1:30 a.m. We were tired, hungry, and in need of sleep. But all I could think about was a blown opportunity to spend quality time with Chinadoll, not to mention the prize between her legs as I was super horny having waited a whole month since our last intercourse. I got home shortly after 2:30 a.m. and went straight to bed.

I awoke mid-morning and immediately called Chinadoll to inform her about our disastrous night. Surprisingly, I sensed doubt as I was providing detail of the occurrences. I was astounded by her attitude, not ever having lied to her in the past. Where was all this negativity coming from? I wondered. Immediately, my mind switched to her friend Miss Celie. After getting dressed I made my way to Chinadoll's house. I greeted her with a hug and kiss as I always did, but couldn't help but feel some rejection. She accused me of having an affair with Manda, whom she had never met, and insinuated that our breakdown was a lie and that I was in town spending time with another woman.

"That's absurd," I said angrily. "I have been faithful to you since the day we met and that's a fact! Never have I contemplated giving you up for anyone."

After reassuring her of my devoted love she revealed that her friend, as I had suspected, suggested to her that I was cheating, basing her assumption primarily on information received from a friend who attended the same college.

"I don't give a damn what her friend said, I know what I've been doing and cheating isn't it!" I shouted. "I refuse to stand here and defend myself against accusations that aren't true."

I then suggested that we confront her friend and her friend's friend to resolve the issue. "That Miss Celie has been a thorn in my ass since the day we met. She's either jealous of you or wants me for herself, and the latter is definitely out of the question. Or, perhaps she wants you Chinadoll for herself," I retorted. "Anyway I've had enough of this nonsense so I'm leaving. I will see you later, that's if it is all right with you?"

As I turned to leave she held my hand, pulled me toward her and kissed me, then assured me that she would see me later.

That evening I returned to find the sweet, humble girl I'd enjoyed over the past two years. We decided to go out for pizza, which was in my favor because that gave me the opportunity to re-visit my favorite spot. Feeling the need to gain as much private time as possible, I ordered take-out. I really needed to be alone with her as I felt her confidence in me slipping away. I was convinced that was largely due to peer pressure. I definitely didn't want that to happen because I truly loved her. I understood her feelings since I was away at school surrounded by so much temptation while she was stuck at home waiting and wondering. I did my best to explain to her that as long as we stuck together and maintained faith and trust in each other and God, nothing and no one could come between us. Then I expressed that a friend was not a friend if they did things to deliberately hurt you or destroy that which made you happy.

"If she was really your friend she would be encouraging, knowing that you love me, instead of discouraging," I said.

Appearing satisfied with our discussion Chinadoll expressed positive words of love as a rebuttal. Offering no resistance to my touches I quickly gained confidence as I carefully and slowly caressed her body until she reached a slow simmer. I kissed her all over lightly, exploring every sensitive spot before coming to rest on her most excitable spot, causing her temperature to reach its boiling point.

Grabbing my long, hard cock she pulled me close and forced it deep inside her; she then locked her legs around my waist and started to fuck my brains out. Exhausted, but not finished, we ate cold pizza in between hot pussy as we fucked the night away.

Manda and I decided to catch the 11 p.m. Greyhound bus back to school Sunday night. That was fine with me because it provided an opportunity for me to spend more quality time with Chinadoll.

I left her house at 9:30 p.m. in order to be on time. The bus was virtually empty so Manda and I sat apart, giving us more space to stretch out and sleep.

The temperature inside and out was cold so I covered myself with a large coat I'd brought. After a hectic weekend, I fell asleep quite easily. During the night, unknown to me, Manda moved next to me as the bus started to get full. For whatever reason, I awoke in a daze facing her with her wig removed. Until then, I had no idea she wore a wig; seeing that gorilla-looking face with that bald head sent me into hysteria. I started screaming, "A monster! A monster!" as I tried to get up and run.

Manda grabbed me then pushed me back into the seat and said, "Shut the hell up you fool and don't start no shit!" At which time she put her wig back on.

"Is that better?" she asked.

I responded with a thank you as we both went back to sleep. I teased Manda most of the time but somehow she loved me as a brother and since she was so sweet and nice, I cherished our friendship. We were always there for each other.

Returning to school I found myself often worrying about Chinadoll and what really was going on inside her head. I had immensely enjoyed our relationship over the past two years and had no problem being faithful to her. She had become the engine behind my desire to succeed. My love for her was enormous but certain inconsistencies in her behavior were eating at my gut, and for the first time, for as long as I could remember, my inner strength was being threatened.

Lil Jet, as we called him, had become my best friend on campus. He was small in stature so I could understand the Lil, but I never knew where the Jet came from and surprisingly I never asked. However, he and I clicked from day one as we shared the same interest; academics, sports and the same taste in women.

It just so happened that Jet and his girlfriend of three years were having major problems. Unlike mine, his problems were much more real since his lady was on campus with him in plain view. He was suffering greatly. I tried my best to ease his pain just by being there as a friend, listening and offering positive advice as we hung out. That was new grounds for me because I had never had my heart broken the way he had, so my words of comfort were based on pure logic. I opened up to him as he had to me, revealing all that had gone on with Chinadoll the past weekend and before. In the end, we realized we were unable to predict future behavior so our brilliant strategy was to just hope and pray. As I saw it, I needed hope that my honey wouldn't cheat or leave me and he needed to pray that his honey would stop cheating and stay with him. We both became bewildered the more we tried to understand the workings of the female mind. In conclusion, Jet and I made what I thought was the best decision ever, and that was to take it one day at a time, doing the best we could.

***

The holiday season was here again. That Thanksgiving Chinadoll had dinner with my family. She was equally as nervous as I was the first time I had dinner at her house but she got through it. We enjoyed the Thanksgiving weekend, rekindling our love every opportunity we had.

Before I knew it I was back home for Christmas and looking forward to spending three weeks with my baby. Leading up to Christmas day Chinadoll and I did a lot of things together, mainly shopping for gifts. Also, we spent time going to movies or just sitting around her house playing with each other in every way.

The big day came and everyone was excited about exchanging presents. That night everyone except for her father retired early to bed after an exhausting day. He left at twilight shortly after dinner to visit his other family. Early in our relationship I had often wondered why he was seldom home and why he spent so little time with his family on holidays. But then I began to hear and see things that confirmed my suspicions. I learned that he had a girlfriend across town with whom he had another set of kids. So from that I gathered that he had to share his time in order to keep things peaceful, not to mention hush-hush. To his credit, I must say he showed respect, if there was such a word when one was practicing infidelity, by always coming home at a reasonable hour.

Be as it may, he treated me good, therefore he was alright with me. I learned never to ask questions or discuss the topic. The point was that everyone was asleep except her father who was not at home, which meant that we would have to wait for his return before we could make love. I felt better knowing he was upstairs where I could hear him before he started downstairs. The floors were wood and made a squeaky noise whenever stepped on. That had become my security system and had yet to fail me. I was as much tuned in to the sound of the floor as I was to the moans of Chinadoll as she moved under me. In the past we had had too many close calls when someone entered the back door without us hearing them. So, in the meantime we kissed and petted as I kept that pussy primed until the right time.

Bingo! I heard the keys jingling at the back door. Dad was home and in a few minutes the game, our love session, would begin. I was thinking, ladies and gentlemen, it's booty time!

Her dad was as predictable as the clock on the wall. Always home before the clock struck 10. With one exception he never awoke to return downstairs. I guess that younger woman wore his ass out. He was probably 20 years her senior and we all know that good, young pussy will put a man into a deep-sleep mode.

I had a good hour and fifteen minutes to get busy. Relocating ourselves to the couch next to the stairs I pulled down Chinadoll's soft, cotton pajamas slipping them off her feet. As I entered her wetness I whispered, "To you I give this gift for life."

"Thank you," she replied.

Slowly I made love to her as she came several times. I found myself not wanting to cum until the last possible minute. Changing positions, she got on her knees as I stroked my dick in her from behind and penetrated deep with long, slow strokes. Sensing the time and feeling that I could no longer hold my passion, I switched her back to her original position. Raising her legs, I buried myself deep inside, feeling my nuts banging against her ass. The sensation became uncontrollable as she matched me stroke for stroke. Feeling me growing inside her she pumped up the pussy as she begged me to give her all of my juice. I exploded, jerking helplessly as cum pumped from my nuts into her. The day had started well and had ended even better. She was happy, I was happy and my friend dick was happy. Boy did I feel on top of the world.

New Year's Eve turned out to be a family affair with everyone sitting around talking, waiting for the clock to strike midnight. I was allowed to remain over to celebrate the New Year with my sugar plum. I couldn't even think about sex with all the people around so I just tried to eat up all the brownies. Knowing that New Year's Day would be different without the crowd, I was patient.

The next day when I arrived at Chinadoll's house I was surprised to find her home alone. Taking advantage of our time alone we wasted no time making love. We spent the rest of the day playing music and talking.

Later that night we went to the movies to see a horror film. The white couple sitting in front of us was quite terrified, with the boyfriend being most afraid. As the music got louder leading up to the scary part I waited until the highlight of the action and screamed, grabbing the white boy's shoulder. He screamed, his girlfriend screamed, and he pissed all over himself. Chinadoll and I were dying laughing. He got mad and started talking smart so I stood up and said, "Bring it on white boy." Well, I guess he didn't want to go there because they left. Everyone around us was laughing because it really was a joke. The urine smell was fresh, causing everybody to make obscene remarks as they left.

The night before I was to return to school Chinadoll informed me that the same guy had called her several times during the holidays.

"Why did you wait until now to tell me?" I asked, feeling a bit upset.

"I was afraid you would go after him," she responded.

"You damn right I would have gone after him! But you told me that you had everything under control. Did you talk to him?"

She said, "Yes."

"Well, no wonder he's calling, and obviously you want him to call. You keep talking to him!" I shouted at her angrily. I received no verbal response as tears started to build up in her eyes.

"I have to go, but I'll call before I leave in the morning," I said as I turned to leave. I felt very angry with her but got over it quickly as I believed in our love.

Back on campus Jet and I hooked up at my crib where we hung-out discussing the happenings of the holiday. I brought up my conversation with Chinadoll the last night I was home. I felt bad when he informed me that his girlfriend Renar had terminated their relationship and had spent the entire Christmas with her new boyfriend. The more he talked about it his mouth began to tremble, accompanied by a constant stream of tears. His pain was greater than any I had ever observed. He expressed how much he loved her and how he had invested his life into their relationship.

Immediately, I started to think about my courtship with Chinadoll. Before long I was crying, as his pain suddenly became mine. The thought of my relationship with Chinadoll going sour was unbearable. But in truth, I was just sharing the pain of a friend. There was no better friend than Jet. Knowing him as I did, I was sure he wasn't ready to give up on her just yet, so I commissioned myself to being there for him during his troubled times as I knew he would do the same for me.

The following evening Jet asked me to go with him to Renar's dorm to discuss the possibility of reconciliation. As I saw it she had already made it final by spending Christmas and New Year's with the starting quarterback of the football team. But I loved Jet as a brother so I smothered my true feelings to support him.

As we were approaching her dorm from one direction, we saw Renar and the ballplayer coming from a different direction, causing a head-on collision or should I say confrontation. Noticing that they were holding hands as they walked toward us put the frame around the picture that had long been completed; at least in my eyes anyway.

Jet definitely wasn't a fighter. As we met at the vertex of pain, Jet asked Renar if he could speak with her. She obliged and the two of them moved away to speak privately. I positioned myself in a way so that there would be no mistake as to my presence. Renar was merciless as she crushed his every thought of ever having a future with her.

Death came quick and swift, and was everything except painless. At that moment I hurt for Jet but admired Renar's courage the way she cut the head off the wounded. That had come to be Jet's saddest hour. I offered encouragement, assuring him that his true love lay in his future. I knew there was no immediate comfort. Renar and her friend walked toward their future, leaving Jet behind to attend to his wounds.

With tears in his eyes he said, "Pook, it hurts...my heart is bleeding. What am I going to do?"

"Deal with the pain one day at a time," I responded.

Over the next week or so my main focus was helping Jet get through his troubled time, which caused me to lose focus on my own situation. Suddenly, I realized that I had not received a letter from Chinadoll since my return to campus. Calling home was difficult because my finances were zero, not to mention that I didn't have a phone in my apartment. Not having much choice I scraped up enough change to make the call. It was very cold outside so I bundled up in my heavy coat and walked down the hill to the phone booth at the corner. Tallahassee to me was the coldest place on earth. But hell, all of my winters were spent in St. Petersburg, Florida, better known as the old folks burial ground. They all came south to St. Petersburg for the winter to die rich. Anyway, I endured Jack Frost and made the call finding Chinadoll's mood pleasant; however, less exhilarating than I had hoped for. As always I expressed how much I loved her. I assured her that she was my soul mate and the only female in the world I wished to spend my life with.

She offered no guarantee of her love, which in the past was automatic. She insisted that we needed to talk so I told her that I would be home the following weekend. After hanging up, thoughts started running through my head like wildfire. Thoughts of a life without Chinadoll was something I had never envisioned. After seeing my friend Jet whom I saw as a strong black man, wither under the power of a woman, I knew only God could help me. Through Jet's pain I had come to understand that it was not who you love but rather who loves you. My inner strength was preparing its defense, sensing that I was about to lose my love.

I arrived home that Friday night and immediately went to Chinadoll's house. I didn't even take the time to hug or converse with my mother. Whether she understood or not didn't matter because my heart was already palpitating to the drums of a death ceremony.

Slightly nervous, but under control, I entered Chinadoll's domain to hear her opening statement and all that was to follow. She was gentle, somewhat nervous, but wasted no time to inform me of the uncertainty of her love. I begged her to tell me what the problem was. In my own heart I knew that I'd done everything right, giving her the best that I had. I'd put her first in every way, never once denying her of anything that her heart desired.

"Why have we reached the crossroads of our relationship? I asked. "Haven't I given you my heart, body and soul?"

"Yes you have," she responded, then went on to say that it had nothing to do with me.

"If it has nothing to do with me then what or who is it?" I inquired and insisted that she answer.

"It's me being here lonely while you are up there with all those college girls," she said.

I responded harshly, "Don't you dare try and put the blame on me because for two-and-a-half years I've cherished and honored you without any questions or serious thoughts of having an affair. You may not love me anymore but I refuse to allow you to make me the scapegoat." Feeling as though I was at war with myself I decided to leave to salvage the remains of our relationship.

For the first time since our union I came and left without any affection. The absence of sex was not what bothered me; it was the disappearance of affection. I was aware I was not to be blamed, but the one thing I learned from Jet's horror was that pain didn't always attack the guilty or perhaps in this case the one who called it quits. More often the recipient of pain was innocent and in time, succumbed to love's blind justice.

That night while lying in my bed unable to sleep, I knew it was over, but I was no quitter. I would fight until I had exhausted all possibilities to save what was once my future, my life. The more thinking I did, the more my pillow got soaked from the tears of a hurt and weary man. On guts and past glory I still felt there was an outside chance I could win, even in a game where I had no vote. I cried and finally drifted off into a restless sleep only to awake in the morning with the same suffering on my mind. My mother knew something was wrong but withheld comments, I guess sensing the pain I was in.

That afternoon I went to see Chinadoll, hoping the nightmare was over. The doom of the day came when I walked into the house. Seeing the look on her mother's face all but summed up my fall from power. For whatever reason, I never felt that she liked me a lot. I was smart enough to know that she had a hand in Chinadoll's decision because there was no way her father would approve of her actions. Also, I observed that last night he had not come home at his usual time. My instincts told me that it had something to do with what was going on with me and Chinadoll. I was his boy; we were cut from the same log. Chinadoll had revealed to me that there was trouble in paradise but would not admit that I was the reason. I guess her mother thought that if Chinadoll got rid of me she wouldn't end up with a man like her father.

After a couple of hours I noticed that her mother hung around much more than usual, pretending to be doing things and asking for Chinadoll's help. I offered to go so that she could assist her mom. She quickly agreed.

At home I kept an aloof manner, avoiding anyone that would ask questions or interfere with the situation unfolding. Before going back to Chinadoll's house my mom suggested that I eat dinner, which she had prepared, so we ate together. Dinner was good but the sadness I was experiencing kept me from enjoying it. My mom didn't say much and I appreciated her for giving me space to deal with my problem.

A solitary feeling overcame me as the walk to Chinadoll's house seemed longer than usual. Entering her house I felt a mean-spirited coldness like none I had ever experienced before, not with her or anyone else. For some strange reason, on that night the house almost seemed ghostly. After inquiring as to the whereabouts of her family members she informed me that her father was out and that the rest of her family was upstairs. Feeling as if I should test her heart I grabbed her hand and pulled her close to me. As

I tried to kiss her she stated that she didn't want to but she allowed me to anyway. I knew from her response that there was little chance of making love that night so I calmed my hormones to be considerate of what she was going through.

"What's wrong?" I asked.

"Nothing."

"You know I'm hurting over the way things are."

"I know, and I don't mean to hurt you."

"Then why are you doing this to us?"

"You know why."

"I know what you said, but I don't understand why you are throwing away all the love we've shared."

"It's hard to explain, but I feel the need to make a change."

"But why change something that has been so good?" I asked with teary eyes.

"I'm lonely and can't handle it anymore."

"But you're not alone. I come home as often as I can."

"I know that, but I need more."

"I only have two more years in school and after that we will have a lifetime together. A good life and we'll never have to be apart again."

"I'm sorry, but my mind is made up. I want to be with Gerold."

"Fuck Gerold! I have given you almost three years of my life and now you come telling me about some motherfucking Gerold? Is this what I deserve for all the love I have given you?"

She remained silent.

"Do you love me?"

"Yes, but I'm not in love with you anymore."

I stood motionless, staring at her through water-soaked eyes, unable to speak. My thoughts swerved toward Gerold. If I had kicked that motherfucker's ass the first time she told me about him I might not have been in this fix, I thought. But that wasn't my style. At that point, I felt as if I was fighting for my life. My whole body was overpowered with sadness. All of the joy that the relationship had brought me over the years suddenly ceased to exist. My body shut down, leaving me without control of my emotions. In the past I had always been able to conceal my true feelings but that time the pain was too great. My manhood was wounded. I was losing a battle I never thought I would be fighting. But I was a real black man, strong, determined and willing to do whatever was necessary by any means possible to win my baby back. I gathered my composure looked her in the eye and said, "I love you. Always will." Then I walked out.

CHAPTER 18

DEALING WITH THE PAIN

Loving Chinadoll was proving to be an uphill climb to the bottom. I was going nowhere fast. For the second night in a row I got little or no sleep and for the first time in my life I had a front-row seat watching the horrors of love unfold. My whole body was under seige from the attack of insomnia, challenging my inner strength. My spirit had been broken but my will as a man was still intact.

Even though sharing the future with Chinadoll appeared bleak, I knew that I couldn't go on until I made my last stand. I decided that no matter what happened the next day I would return the following weekend in final defense of my reign. The picture was already completed but the frame was not in place. A quitter I wasn't and she was too special to give up without a fight. I just hoped and prayed that in the end if I couldn't save the relationship I could make it through what was to be the worse time of my life. As I lay in bed unable to sleep, I prayed that God would remove the insomnia to allow me some peace so I could drift into a place where there was no pain.

I awoke feeling exhausted. Stress had zapped my energy. My subconscious had voted not to see Chinadoll prior to leaving as I had been stripped of my ability to fight. My only course of action was to lie around most of the day hoping to be able to at least take a nap until it was time for me to leave for school. I thought it best that I left early that afternoon; however, I called Chinadoll just to say once again that I still loved her and to let her know that I was coming back next week to resolve the issue. Her response was that her mind was made up. My last words were, "I'll see you next weekend."

After arriving back at my apartment I found my sleep pattern to be much the same, little or no sleep. That evening I found Jet sitting alone in the student union game room. His suffering had not subsided much but seeing me seemed to lift his spirit. I spent little time talking about my situation; instead, I focused on how he was handling his. He expressed that he had feelings of withdrawal and depression and was unable to concentrate on school. I still felt that I had one glimmer of hope so there was no need for me to panic as of yet. Jet needed my encouragement and support if he was going to get through his predicament. So for the rest of the week I was going to get him involved in any and everything necessary to get his mind off of Renar. I knew a little honey nicknamed Red from Pensacola, Florida who had been admiring him from a distance so I got him to walk over to the freshman dorm for a hook up. They were not strangers to each other. It was just that the timing was never right, especially while Renar was the head bitch in charge.

Once Red came outside I generated enough conversation to make them both feel comfortable then I split. Knowing that he liked her made it easy for me to pull it off, and when I saw the smile on his face I knew at least for the moment there would be some joy. The remainder of the evening I spent alone trying to smother the pain smoldering deep inside me. I had been witness to Jet's anguish over the past months and expected that my own agony would be equally as bad should things not go well upon my return home. The Chinadoll dilemma was consuming 100% of my brain power. I no longer had control over my thoughts, whether for the class lecture period or during free time.

School and everything else became a distant second to Chinadoll. I was suspended somewhere in its abyss.

That year on my birthday, February 1, 1970, also was the day that would decide the rest of my life. I had made arrangements with a friend to travel home early. My plan was to get there before dusk to allow enough time to get really spiffed up. During our trip I elected not to divulge what was going on between me and Chinadoll. That way no explanation would be required during the return expedition.

I arrived home earlier than anticipated. My mom was expecting me and had cooked dinner. Eating was a must on that night. It would surely help a stomach already boiling of pure acid. Subsequent to dinner I took a long, hot bath, hoping to calm my nerves. Afterwards I lotioned my body real good, brushed my teeth then followed up with a straight shot of Listerine. I didn't want Chinadoll to smell nothing but goodness coming from me.

Since it was my birthday I had hopes of celebrating with Chinadoll, so I dressed for the occasion by putting on my salt and pepper pants, black shoes and socks, a blue shirt, a black double-breasted blazer, and a tie that brought out everything I had on. I was clean down to the bone.

"Hot damn, I'm cleaner than a sweet dick dog," I said while looking in the mirror. Shortly after I had finished glutting over myself, reality reappeared. The horror of what could happen was once again upon me. Be as it may, I was off to face the demons nesting inside my soul. I walked slower than usual that night trying to prepare myself for the worst, while hoping for the best.

When I arrived on the porch I took a deep breath then rang the doorbell. When Chinadoll opened the door I saw Gerold sitting on the sofa in the dimly lit corner of the room on the same couch I had used innumerable times to make love to her. At that moment my heart exploded. A fire hydrant of tears opened in an attempt to drown the sorrows of the wreck. I was lifeless.

Nothing existing on God's earth could have prepared me for that degree of pain. And for the first time since the whole mess began, I thought death would have been an easier way out. With what willpower I had left I looked through teary eyes straight into her eyes and asked, "Is this really what you want?"

"Yes," she replied.

"Fine! I'll leave but no matter what I will never come back again," I retorted. Then I continued in a more gentle tone, "No one on the face of this earth could love you as much as I do." I turned and walked away. With a steady stream of tears running down my face I began to sing:

> *Sunshine blue sky please go away.*
> *My girl have found another and she's*
> *gone away. With her went my future,*
> *my life is filled with gloom. Day*
> *after day I keep locked up in my room.*
> *I know to you it might sound strange*
> *but I wish it would rain ah! Ya! Ya!*

After singing that chord a few times the Lord granted my wish as it began to rain lightly. I smiled through a mist of tears as I thanked him for carrying me. I was relying totally on His strength as I bore witness to the changing of the guard.

I was a weary man walking everywhere but going nowhere for what seemed like forever that night. I couldn't seem to stop crying. I was unable to understand how I could love her so and give so much and yet lose her. It just didn't seem fair. I deserved better. I continued walking for hours, all that time in a slow drizzle of rain that I appreciated because it helped to soothe my aching heart.

That was my 20th birthday. I was supposed to be celebrating, having a good time, but that was not to be…not that night at least. Instead, that night became the darkest of all times. Where was her compassion? I asked myself. Better still, where was my thinking? I was aware one week ago that the picture had been completed. Fuck the frame! The picture was the same whether the frame was around it or not. Who was I kidding? The bitch had made it crystal clear that she didn't want me anymore so whatever fucking pain I was having on my birthday I damn well deserved it. I could have been in Tallahassee with my dick stuck a mile in one of them bitches' ass. But noooo! I had to give it one last chance. Dumb ass!

Fury built inside of me the more I realized that I was the fool for loving her so deeply. At an instant I wanted to kick his ass and her ass too. Failing to pay attention to where I was walking I found myself in unfamiliar territory within a white neighborhood. I continued walking, changing direction until I came upon familiar ground. The project where I lived was just down the street but I decided to venture down the road where I knew Gerold would walk en route home.

It was about eleven o'clock so I figured he should be coming by soon. The longer I waited the madder I got. I waited for more than an hour but that dickhead never showed up. I figured Chinadoll had her mother take him home knowing that I would kick his ass. I wasn't mad at him because of the woman, I just wanted to put my foot in his ass on general principle.

By now I was soaking wet and that dap-daddy outfit I was wearing had shrunken six inches. I had lost my woman and the only dress clothing I had. I was pissed! "Some motherfucker got to pay, especially for my new outfit," I retorted loudly.

I made up my mind that night that if it took the rest of my life I would seek revenge on both of them. My vengeance would be cruel. I wouldn't rest until they had been made to feel pain two times greater than what I was feeling, I promised myself.

It was shortly after midnight when I arrived home. My mother was already in bed, which was a good thing. That way I didn't have to answer any questions about my night or my being wet. Again I took a hot bath, but that time to just feel better as my life at that point was in shambles. Still crying, I prayed for comfort. With the help of God Almighty, I began to experience some freedom. Whoever said that a man shouldn't cry obviously hadn't felt the wrath of a woman or experienced her wickedness. Surprisingly, I suppose from exhaustion I was able to fall asleep.

I awoke late the following morning with puffy, bloodshot eyes. My mom was already downstairs and there was no way scars from such a horrendous night could be hidden. I decided to take it on the chin and tell her that Chinadoll and I had broken up. She listened attentively without interrupting. After I finished spilling my guts she responded, "I'm sorry to hear. She was a nice girl." Then went on to say, "I know that you loved her very much but in life these things do happen." At the point of her stating how much I loved her, tears began to flow as if they had never stopped from the night before. I could tell that she was hurting also, for me I suppose, as her eyes became misty.

She was able to fight back her tears but there was no shut-off valve to mine.

"Let this be a lesson that the only person that you can control is yourself. There's never a guarantee that another individual will love you as much as you do or just because you love them or vice-versa," my mom said. "The truth of the matter is that I've known for some time that there was trouble in paradise," she continued.

I'm thinking, if you knew, why in the hell did you let me make a damn fool of myself? But then I realized that sometimes you have to go alone. I must say that I felt relieved that my mom knew; however, I felt no relief from the pain of losing my woman.

The rest of the day I sat around trying to convince myself that everything would be all right. I knew when I left Chinadoll last night that I could withstand this bombshell no matter the pain. My agony was a result of truly loving her and not because I was less of a man. So I chilled the rest of the day while mentally preparing myself for the long journey back. I kept wondering how one repairs a heart so badly damaged. The more I accepted the reality of the situation the more confident I became. I might have hurt for an extensive period, but I was never one to cry long over spilled milk. It was done and there was nothing I could do about it, at least not then. Every dog has his day and I should have mine.

In a town of beautiful women I had failed to maintain my reserve. I had entrusted my life to one beautiful woman. I had been bamboozled into thinking that love lasts forever. I came to realize that forever is for as long as you want them or as short as they don't want you. I had no thoughts or desires of seeing nor having another woman at that time. My heart came without a crutch and the first-aid bandages were all used up last night, without success I might add. So there was nothing left for me to do except recuperate and rehabilitate slowly. Besides, my dick wouldn't get hard if I stuck it in a block of ice. I was reminded that this was the first time since ninth grade that my pole wasn't waxed on my birthday. Isn't that the fucking blues? She could have at least fucked me on my birthday and quit me the next day.

That had been the most miserable weekend of my life, and I was afraid that the worst was yet to come. If there was a good side to this it was that I was back on campus with my #1 ace spoon coon who just happened to be suffering from the same illness. The lovebug had a choke hold on Jet and me. I wasted no time looking up my boy as I needed counseling. I knew that he was still going through his crisis but fuck that, I needed his shoulder to cry on because my shit was fresh and I was hurting worse than a knock-kneed bitch having a baby.

After class Jet and I decided to get something to eat. It was early so the restaurant was almost empty. That allowed me to open up and talk freely about the past weekend. I started at the point of how well I was dressed; walking him step-by-step through that night, not leaving out any details. Tears began to form as I was telling the story. Before I could finish, I'd be damned if Jet wasn't crying harder than I was. I was thinking, what the fuck is going on? This is my time to weep!

So I asked him if he was alright. He said, "As you was telling me what took place all I could think about was the football player's dick hung all up in Renar."

Then I started boo-hooing as I thought about Gerold's little midget-dick up in Chinadoll. Until then I had managed not to think along those lines and now my friend had me thinking of shit I really didn't need in my head. Now I was truly fucked up inside. Here we were in a restaurant crying, nose dripping, trying to eat a greasy cheeseburger with fries—the blind leading the cripple, both crazy in love with another man's pussy.

Things went on that way for the entire winter term. Both Jet and I were unable to focus on school. Our wounds just didn't seem to be healing fast enough. Time appeared to be the only remedy. All I did was stay home and listen to Isaac Hayes's, *Hot Butter and Soul* album. I played it over and over until the grooves were almost worn through, wearing out a brand new needle. The song that soothed my soul the most was, *I don't know what to do with myself*.

> *I don't know what to do with myself*
> *I don't know just what to do with myself*
> *No one to talk to, No one to hold*
> *No one to soothe my soul*
> *I'm tired and misused…so confused*
> *Feelings going 'round and 'round*
> *Spirits are going down and down*
> *Half a man-trying to understand*

I remember sitting in physics class during final exam, unequipped to perform any task except put my name on the test sheet, which I did from habit. That grading period I dropped below C-average for the first time in my life and yes, I received a "F" in physics. Jet fared no better as he did poorly in a couple of subjects. In every way, I became disappointed with myself. I had to convince myself that I couldn't afford to continue down that path of self-destruction.

One day Jet and I were chilling at my crib with our blues on, eating southern fried fish and sipping on Cream White Concord wine. Displeased with who I had become, I reached deep within my soul, tapping all the inner strength I could muster. I decided that day I wasn't going to cry anymore. I'd finally realized that the hardest thing to do was love someone that couldn't be true and even harder than that, was to love someone that didn't love you. Both Jet and I were guilty of the latter and had paid a terrible price for something as simple as being in love. I told Jet of my feelings which he shared and agreed to. Together we vowed that we would wreak havoc on the female population forever from that day forward. On that day the slut puppy was born.

My ability to love had been eradicated from my body by a female who had no compassion for the words love, commitment and trust. All of which I honored when I gave my heart, body and soul to Chinadoll. All I got in return was somebody's dick in my pussy. Now it was my turn and I would fuck over the females of the world. No matter if they were single, married, or other. I would make them love me, but their love would be futile. I would fuck them every which way but loose and then move on to the next victim. One thing I had learned was that if you can't love you won't be hurt. I would never suffer that degree of pain ever again, for love was no longer a part of my gender.

My game was a little rusty after being with Chinadoll for two-and-a-half years. Before becoming pussy religious (that's when you dedicate your dick to one female) I'd learned who to prey on. So I decided to opt for the gullible prey first. I figured instant success would be a confidence builder.

First on my hit list was my homegirl Jadie who was in her freshman year at FAMU. She was interested in me during my high school years and had made it clear since being in college that she was mine whenever I was ready.

When I first met her she wasn't allowed to take company. Her mother was one of those evil, mean and nasty women who kept all her daughters inside under lock and key. There was no way I was going to waste time or energy trying to seduce her. Once I started dating Chinadoll the risk was too great and she was never thought of again, until now. There was no risk now as I had nothing left to lose. Her willingness made it easy to schedule time with her.

I made contact the following day and invited her over to my apartment. She showed up promptly and welcomed a kiss on the cheek. She smiled in appreciation, like a kid in a candy store for the first time. My plan was to sit and talk on a couple of visits, making sure I said all the right things. That night was a lot of fun. We played and laughed while lying on my bed watching television. To gain her trust I purposely avoided making any sexual advances, however, upon her request I allowed her to lie comfortably in my arms. I kept my show of affection above the neck while kissing from time to time. From her reactions I knew she wanted more but I wanted her to slow roast for a while.

Jadie came over the next evening after school and prepared a delicious dinner for both of us. Subsequent to the meal we kicked back on the couch and watched a movie. Again I made no attempts to seduce her. She was in my Crock-Pot simmering for sexual delight. It was Thursday; Saturday would be my day.

There was no school, no studying, and absolutely no reason for her not to spend the night. I planned to slow fuck her all night until the chickens in the backyard crowed and she screamed cock-a-doodle to my dick.

On Friday night I hung out alone, scouting the campus for new meat. Jadie wanted to spend time with me but I informed her that I had business. Besides, that bird was already in the bag just waiting to be plucked so there was no need to overdo it.

As usual she arrived right on time and was looking good. Experience had taught me that less food was better when a sexual marathon was about to happen, so I ate at six o'clock to provide sufficient time for the small portion of food to digest. After giving my roommate instructions as to my plans for the night, he left and Jadie and I retired to the room. I put on some jazz and immediately reverted back to my usual self. We kissed as I caressed her body with soft kisses and touches.

I held her hands, not allowing her to give foreplay. I wanted her to experience a real player and she deserved the ultimate fulfillment. Besides, I wanted to pace myself while draining all the fluids from her body. I licked her nipples then touched all her sensitive spots and she came before I mounted her. My refusal to permit her from giving back was driving her wild as I continued to work her hot spots. Her expressions and voice began to change as the demons emerged from overwhelming passion. Aware that she was way past her boiling point, I spread her legs and pushed my cock deep inside her saturated cunt. Clutching me tightly she roared then wrapped her big legs around me and fucked me like I was the last dick on earth. I was stunned.

I had no idea that innocent little girl could fuck like that. If that bitch hadn't locked her legs, my ass would have been bucked off. I gathered myself. Raising her legs high over her head I rammed my cock so deep she gagged. Releasing her legs I changed the rhythm, working my mojo while moving like a yo-yo. She came like a spigot was turned on in her ass.

The night was still young and so far I hadn't cum. That pussy was so good I was beginning to wonder why anyone would want to settle for just one. My destiny was to spread joy and happiness through dicksmanship for I was a true dicksman and my calling was to fuck. After cumming several times, Jadie wanted to rest, but I told her there was no rest for the weary; at least, not until she made Big Poppa cum. I hadn't seen a woman yet that could make me cum. I came when I was ready, so homegirl was in for the long haul. I worked that thing on her a little longer until she became so worn out that rigormortis was about to set up in her ass. Satisfied that I had taken her to a place where no one else could, I came good in her slumbering pussy.

After eating the breakfast that she prepared, Jadie left upon my telling her that I had things to do. I'd met this sweet little honey one Friday night at the club and promised her that I would come over Sunday afternoon. During our conversation at the club, I assessed that it would take about one week to get in her drawers. I planned to charm her during the week and tap her ass on Saturday. In the meantime, I figured I'd spank Jadie's ass Wednesday and Thursday night to keep her satisfied, and me free on Saturday to bang my new tail.

On Saturday evening everything was going according to plan. My new brown sugar had just arrived and my dick was already chuckling. She was dressed in a brown pantsuit with a printed brown-and-beige blouse. The perfume she wore was mild, but sexually arousing. Having zero trust for women, I instructed my roommate to tell Jadie that I went home for the weekend should she come by before he left. I just had the feeling that she would show up even though I told her I wouldn't be home and would see her on Sunday.

My lady and I were chilling in the bedroom listening to soft music. She was a little country girl and kind of shy. I could tell right away she lacked experience in the sexual arena. I thought it would be best to take my time and teach her how to really seduce a man, especially me. I unbuttoned her blouse to undo her brassiere. I started kissing and fondling her breasts very gently, barely touching her nipples. I wanted her to feel the excitement from the energy of my fingertips. I removed all of her clothing except her underwear. Then I removed my own clothes in their entirety. Pointing out each of my sensitive spots I instructed her how to caress them.

"Hold my penis and I will show you how to stroke it," I said. She held it as directed.

"Oh, God! I don't know if I can take this," she whispered.

"Trust me, you'll stretch beyond my size."

At that point there was a knock on the door. The room was completely dark with the curtains drawn so there was no way anyone would know if someone was inside. We lay very still and quiet. The knocking continued for about five minutes. Suddenly, I heard a noise at the window as if someone was trying to look inside. Shortly after that I heard footsteps on the stairs, which were just outside the door. I rushed to the front window to see Jadie walking toward campus. She had become my dick junkie, seeking to reach that first-time high.

Re-entering the room, I noticed my little sweet thing massaging her breasts as she'd been taught. I was impressed, a quick learner. Straddling her body I eased back in the bed but stopped to suck her nipples. I kissed her passionately then licked all around her lips before inserting my tongue into her mouth. She sucked so hard she almost pulled my head into her mouth. I quickly corrected her and explained how it should be done. From the jerk she gave me I realized that she should be sucking on my dick. I guided her mouth to my chest while directing her to duplicate my actions moving from nipple to nipple. I moaned, letting her know how good she was while at the same time positioning her mouth on my cock. That bitch didn't need any training sucking dicks; she was a natural-born sucker.

"Oh, yes!" I screamed. "Suck this dick you bitch." It must have been a fetal thing because this whore was sucking a new pathway to my ass. She was happy because she had found her niche. My niche was fucking and I wanted to fuck because this honey had sucked my dick to twice its size.

I rolled her over on her back, reached for her drawers with both hands as she lifted her ass for ease of removal. I was getting ready to fuck that bitch to death. I threw the panties on the floor with the rest of her shit, spread those legs and, "Oh, my God!" I shouted, as a funk monster jumped out of her pussy, grabbed my throat and damn near choked me to death.

"Bitch, you smell like a buzzard done crawled up your ass and died," I said angrily. "You need to go home and take a motherfucking douche!"

Confused and not really understanding what was wrong she asked, "What's a douche?"

"What's a douche? Didn't your mother teach you anything?" I said as I blew my top, grabbed her clothes with one hand and her arm with the other and put her naked ass outside in the cold.

"Baby, it's cold out here," she cried.

"Don't worry, the cold will freeze the funk," I said, slamming the door.

I was fit to kill. Rushing back into the room I opened the window, rolled up the sheets and threw them into the washer. I was thinking, as I sat down on the couch with my dick staring up at me, that everything that looked good was not always good.

What the hell was I going to do now? Saturday night and I had no pussy. If I hadn't lied to Jadie I would go to her room, bring her back to my crib and fuck the shit out of her. That's what I get for lying, I thought, while looking at the biggest dick I had ever seen. It stayed hard all night, throbbing at the head as if to torment me. I even took a BC powder to help ease the pain; nothing helped. I was one miserable dickhead.

I thought it would be better to wait until early evening to contact Jadie. That way I would eliminate any suspicion as to my being out of town. I stayed home chilling with the same old hard dick that had been bugging me all night.

Not surprisingly, Jadie showed up shortly after noon. She immediately started inquiring about my weekend; wanting to know why I didn't let her know that I was going away. I quickly put a stop to that shit letting her know that she don't check me.

"I go where I want to when I choose to," I said, with that don't ask me no more damn questions look on my face.

Stunned, she responded, "I didn't mean any harm."

"I didn't mean any harm either, now come over here and give Big Poppa some loving."

With a smile on her face, homegirl moseyed on over and sat on an already hard dick. We kissed softly as I let her know how much I missed her that weekend. My roommate was gone so we went straight to the bedroom where I played in that pussy until curfew time. I walked with her just to the back of the dorm, pausing for a hug and kiss along the way to make her feel special. Without venturing to the front of the dorm where all eyes would be on us I said good night as I stroked her cunt telling her to keep it warm for me.

"I will Baby because you know this is all yours with a lot of love."

Walking away I was thinking, who does that bitch think she's talking to—all mine until you want to fuck another nigga—and don't ever talk to me about that love bullshit. I never will fall for that dumb shit again. Chinadoll had destroyed all of my faith when it came to the two-legged devil.

Walking back to my apartment I mumbled to myself that the only thing I wanted to feel was a hard dick cumming in a tight pussy. So love me if you want to, but you'd be in the love boat all by your lonesome because I would fuck you until the next fine ass came along.

CHAPTER 19

ULTIMATE SEX

Somehow Zill got my address and wrote to tell me that she would be in Tallahassee the following weekend. Yes, that was the same Zill that knocked out Zass in the first round at the opening bell during the beach party. She was a good friend and lots of fun so I looked forward to seeing her. Just the kind of person I needed to see after what I'd been through with Chinadoll.

She arrived at my apartment before noon that Saturday morning; I wasn't expecting her until later that afternoon. When I answered the door I was wearing nothing but my gym shorts. To be polite I suggested that I would put on something more appropriate, but she insisted that I need not bother, especially if I was comfortable because she had no problem looking at my fine body.

"If it works for you, it works for me," I said.

We sat for a long while talking about all the things that had taken place since high school. She informed me that she had become pregnant by Zass and had given birth to a son last year. Further, she enlightened me to the fact that she and Zass had broken up and for the time being she and her son were living with her grandparents in a small town 30 miles south of Tallahassee. It was early evening when she indicated that she had to leave. She had promised her granddad that she'd be home before 8 p.m.

The following Tuesday afternoon she came over as she had promised. I was still not completely over Chinadoll and from time to time I caught myself singing my down-home favorite *I just don't know what to do with myself.* Zill heard me singing and requested that I sing the whole song for her. She insisted that I sounded very good. She was funny and crazy as we laughed and talked, just having a good time. Before we realized it we found ourselves in each others arms. We went to the bedroom and got undressed while kissing and caressing each other. She lay on the bed with me on top of her. I quickly noticed that the sensation was causing rapid communication between my brain and my dick. She was quiet, but oh my God was she good! She had natural rhythm like no other before her. I had never been sexed so good.

"Baby, I can't hold it," I said.

"That's OK, go ahead and wet this pussy."

"Oh, Baby, this pussy is so good."

"Do you like what I do to you?"

"Oh, yes! Oh, shit! Oh, Baby...Oh, Baby...Oh, Baby. No one can make me cum this good."

For the first time in my life I lost total control as I came at her will and not mine. She kept me hard all evening with me loving every minute. I could see why Zass took all the ass whippings from her, I'd take one myself for that pussy, I smiled.

"Good, God Almighty, that bitch took me to another level of fucking," I said silently.

Zass and I had considered ourselves to be cousins, but cousin or no cousin I had to have that fine thing in my bed at any cost. I didn't care if he found out because I already knew that I was going to chase this one from now on.

I thought about the cigarette commercial...*I'll walk a mile for a Camel.* Well, I would walk 10 miles for that pussy. It was just that good. After she left I lay naked in the bed

155

with a hard-on thinking, Chinadoll had my heart but Zill had my dick.

Changing the words to my favorite song I sang, *I may not know what to do with myself, but I sure know what to do with my dick....keep it regularly in Zill's ass.* They should have named her rhythm in motion I thought, just before dropping off to a happy sleep.

Zill was unable to come to Tallahassee the following weekend so I decided to go and visit her. I didn't have a car so I paid one of my homeboys to take me to the nearest crossroad to where she lived. It was about 10 miles away according to the directions she gave. Without hesitation I started walking down the long, narrow road. After walking one-third of the way a man in a truck loaded with chickens offered me a ride, which I gladly accepted. It was shortly past noon when I arrived. Her family was about to have lunch and invited me to join them. After getting to know her grandparents we walked around the farm and played with her son until dusk. That evening after her son was put down for the night we went to the barn. That was the night of nights. That was the closest I would ever get to heaven, I thought. Whoever was in the haystack before me definitely wasn't looking for a needle.

"There should have been a law against anyone working their ass this good," I told her.

I arrived back at my apartment Sunday evening. I took a shower and retired to bed totally exhausted. With a smile on my face I reminisced about my greatest lovemaking experience. A knock at the door interrupted my thoughts. It was Jadie. I was thinking, as good as her stuff is I don't want no more. Zill is now my thrill on the hill. But I'd learned that you don't fire any of your females because as soon as you did a drought would surely come. Rather than risk not being able to perform up to par I told her that I went home for the weekend and had contracted a stomach virus that caused diarrhea. She felt so sorry for me as I slept in her arms all night. Miraculously, the next morning I had fully recovered.

"Thanks to your loving touch I feel better," I told her, and then went to work on her ass.

Zill called that Monday and informed me that she was moving back home because her mother was ill. Boy, it was a good thing I was nice to Jadie because right about then I would have been up shit creek without a paddle. I was totally dejected and would miss her very much, but summer was just around the corner and I would be home myself. With that bit of information I quickly diverted my attention to Jadie. I wasted no time calling and telling her how sweet she was.

With just a few weeks left in school I needed to make one more score, a little going-home present and something to line up for the fall session. Experience had taught me that you have to keep thinking ahead in order to stay on top. I decided to scheme a bit so I put myself into the path of stink stuff to see if she had discovered what a douche was. She was a very good-looking lady with a supermodel body that made the thought of me not pleasing her hard to bear. She deserved to have me inside her and now that Zill was gone Jadie would need some help. Knowing her schedule and her pattern I appeared in front of her at the right time and place. Showing the humble side of my game I said, "Hi, how are you doing?"

"I'm OK," she responded.

"I've been wanting to talk to you but was a little afraid."

"Afraid of what?" she asked.

"I wasn't too kind the last time we were together and I truly apologize because I really like you a lot."

"I like you too and the things you said were true. Because of that night I've educated myself on proper hygiene. As a result, I feel and smell like a new woman."

Right about then I felt the joy all the way down in my loins; so deep that the mouth of my dick was smiling. I could not display my feelings or emotions because she was being real. I was thinking like the dog that I was, but I understood that compassion was required for this occasion. That evening I prepared a candlelight dinner for two, after which I invited her to spend the night. She was everything I thought she would be. I juggled my time between Jadie and sweet stuff the remainder of the term.

I was back home for the summer and working at my old job; more importantly, Zill was waiting with open arms and legs, and her own apartment. Damn it, I thought, how could one man be so lucky? Boy, if I was still with that no good, cheating-ass Chinadoll the only smell on my dick would be hers and I would have missed out on all the blessings that had been sent my way. Thank the Lord for bitches.

I'd made enough money gambling the last few days of school to put a down payment on a used car. Thanks to Smackie I learned how to cheat at cards well enough to break the unseasoned country boys. My mother cosigned with the understanding that I would make each and every payment on time. I would have rather died than to miss a payment and have Mama to pay because she would have killed me anyway.

The ride gave me unlimited potential. I could search the neighboring towns that had women in each of them without fear of being caught. Oh, what a wonderful world we live in, I thought, while driving in search of new pussy. Knowing that after Chinadoll it was not likely that I would find pure love, I decided to settle for plenty of pussy and to love every minute of it.

I spent my days at work, my evenings scouting for new prey, and my nights trying to fuck Zill to death. It couldn't get much better than this, I thought. Until one day when I was standing in the hallway just outside the lunchroom. Two of God's best creations walked by and sent my ass into a frenzy.

They were equally beautiful with bodies sculptured to complement their evil ways. One was high yellow with sexy bow legs and a tight ass. The other was coal black with cantaloupe breasts and a melon booty. I froze as they walked by smiling, knowing what they had done to me and the other fifty or so men as we all stood hypnotized from the motion of ass swaying.

All I could see at that moment was myself between one of them honey's thighs. Which one didn't matter, I knew the possibility of having both was slim. But I was a man of great faith, believing that anything's possible and would never settle for just one. But for now I had to track the one with the least resistance. Through research I learned that the high-yellow chick had two kids and a crazy man who would kill to keep her. So obviously that situation wasn't the most optimum. The black beauty's name was Karo and she lived with her mother, had a daughter, and no steady man. Bingo!

One Friday night a few weeks later, I found myself in her arms. Karo had been the Homecoming Queen a couple years earlier and as I found out, the pride of her town. Her hometown was definitely different from mine. About 2:30 a.m. as I was leaving her house, 10 dudes who were waiting to kick my ass surrounded my car. I gathered that they were pissed with my coming to their town and courting their most precious. I might have tried two, but not 10, so I backed into the house and told Karo that this was her lucky day because I was spending the night. Since her mother was home the couch was my only option. I left unharmed about 6:00 that morning.

The next afternoon Zill showed up at my house pissed off. My mother was fond of Zill and knew her quite well because her family attended the same church we did. So when Zill appeared angry and hurt my mom was sympathetic and joined in on the crusade at my expense. I just sat there and took it all in, showing respect for my mom's sake. After they finished lecturing me I got dressed then went to Zill's crib. I remained quiet for the duration of the short trip to let her know that I didn't appreciate the grandstanding in the presence of my mother. I quickly dismissed the attitude once inside her crib, especially after she started getting naked. We wasted no time getting into it and made passionate love for what seemed like forever. We made love in every position possible that night until the break of dawn. The sheet and padding were soaked. With neither of us willing to yield in defeat we declared it a draw. The linen was changed and I went out like a light.

I awoke about noon to find Zill absent from the house. Noticing that my car keys were missing I immediately got dressed and went downstairs to check on its whereabouts. One of the guys hanging out in the parking lot informed me that Zill had taken the car. I was madder than a motherfucker as I wondered why she would do such a thing. I made it very clear that she couldn't drive the car since she wasn't covered by the insurance. Besides taking the car, she left her son for me to babysit. She knew I wasn't into babysitting no damn children.

The apartment had no air conditioning and it was hot as hell. It was hotter than a steam room full of black folks. To make matters worse the kid had on a dirty diaper full of shit, which gave off an awful stench and had flies buzzing all around. I had no clue as to how to change a fucking diaper.

Two hours later that bitch came through the door with a smile on her face.

"Wipe that goddamn smile off your face because I didn't put that motherfucker there," I yelled. "You know you don't mess with my shit without my permission!"

"I'll drive our car whenever I damn well please and don't you raise your voice at me!"

I was a bit confused at that moment. "Our, my ass! You don't make no payments on that Chevy Super Sport. This was your last time driving my motherfucking car and I'll raise my voice at your dumb ass whenever the fuck I please," I shouted.

At that moment I had a flashback to the time she dropped Zass with a right cross to the jaw. And as I anticipated, she threw a hard right, which I blocked. I in turn landed an overhand slap that sent her reeling backward for 15 feet.

"This ain't Zass and if you move I'll kick your ass," I shouted at her. As I took my keys I told her not to fuck with me again because I didn't like the fighting. I then directed her to change the baby's shitty diaper.

"See ya!" I said, as I left her house.

That evening I went to Karo's house. Instead of being trapped inside I decided to take her and her daughter for a drive on the beach. Her beautiful dark-chocolate face and pearl-white teeth reminded me of Caramel, prettier, but not quite as fine. But then, no one I knew was as shapely as Miss Caramel. Still, looking at her made me drip the whole night long. I had to be cool because she was no fool and romance was the key to unlocking her thighs. I decided to play the game until the fat lady sang.

Upon returning to her house she informed me that she was getting an apartment of her own. All of a sudden my dick started clapping to the tune the fat lady was singing. Hearing that information I decided that I would spend as much time as possible with Karo prior to the weekend. That way when she moved into her new place my roots would have been planted.

She moved most of the small things on Friday. She didn't have much furniture but she had a king-size bed, which I was quick to set up. By late afternoon that Saturday the apartment was completely set up. I drove her back to her mother's house to get her daughter. Before leaving, she hugged her mother and expressed appreciation for all the help she had given her. I admired her for that.

On the way back we stopped to pick up a pizza. There was something about pepperoni that made my cock hard, but then, it got hard when I ate a hot dog, hamburger, and one time, I remember after eating liver. It must have been the protein.

With her permission I took a shower. After the baby fell asleep Karo made her a nice comfortable pallet on the floor then went to take her bath.

After about fifteen minutes the bathroom door opened. The cloud of vapor hid her from view. Out of the mist she entered the bedroom dressed in a black negligee. I sat in a trance, staring as if I had just seen something out of the ordinary. I was spellbound. At that moment I knew God was a black man and this was his daughter Aphrodite. She was indeed a goddess.

"Are you pleased?" she asked.

"As pleased as my Father was when he rested on the seventh day," I responded.

I stood up to meet her, taking her into my arms and began kissing her passionately. I lifted her luscious body and transported her to the bed. There was no need to rush as we had the night to ourselves. I explored her body with kisses and located all of her sensitive spots. Taking her hand together with mine, we caressed her clitoris until it popped out of its protective shell. I removed her hand to prevent her from masturbating as I sucked softly on her nipples then kissed the inner of her thighs; driving her to hysteria.

She begged me to enter her but I continued to focus on her sensitive areas. Her clitoris had become cherry red and was protruding from a dark-chocolate overlay. Sensing that she was at the point of ultimate ecstasy I parted her legs and eased every inch of my cock deep into her tightly woven body. She gasped, as if unable to make a sound then screamed out loudly in delight. The sound was so profound that it woke the baby momentarily. We remained motionless until her daughter returned to sleep. Continuing our sexual voyage I raised both her legs and slow fucked her with long, easy strokes.

Retracting myself fully, purposely to tease, she cried, "No!" in a soft, demanding voice while grabbing her prize and guiding it to her wet delight. Placing her feet under my knees I stroked her with deep caterpillar moves. Her movements became more vigorous. Releasing her legs she wrapped them around me and fucked my ass until the demons in me came out. I came like a motherfucking dairy cow being milked.

"Girl, you worked that pussy on me!" I said, as we both quickly fell asleep from sexual exhaustion. Everyone should have a night like this, I thought.

The next morning I awoke to find her in my arm with her firm butt tucked snugly between my legs. I got up and went to the bathroom to relieve myself. Becoming aroused again I started the morning just as I had the night before. There were times in my life that I wished would never end, and that was truly one of them.

A few days later my sister introduced me to this sweet darling named Gretta from Mobile, Alabama, who attended junior college with her. She was attractive from head to toe. Good hair, pretty face, gorgeous smile and one fine body. From then on my time was shared between my two love birds, Gretta in the afternoons and early evenings; Karo all night long. They lived 20 miles apart in different cities so there was little chance of anyone finding out about the other.

Things were great until one Saturday afternoon when Zill showed up at my house. Without even knocking she just waltzed in and found Gretta sitting on my lap kissing me. We were in the kitchen so she had to walk about 20 feet to reach us. The closer she got to us the madder she became. I had told Gretta about Zill in order to cover my tracks in case a situation like that occurred.

Everyone knew that Zill was a fighter and crazy. There was no other way for her to be because her mother was just as crazy. Her mother had hit her father with a baseball bat, broke his knee, knocked him through a glass window, and ran over him with the car, breaking his legs. From deductive reasoning I think I could declare her crazy.

But the problem here was that Gretta was a black belt in karate and had no qualms about kicking Zill's ass. To make things worse, Gretta started kissing me fervently. Zill who was now mad enough to kill her mama shouted to Gretta, "What the fuck you doing sitting on my man, bitch?"

Gretta responded, "If he was your man you would be sitting here instead of me, bitch!" She then stood up to a face-off. Before I could stand between them Zill threw a punch that was blocked then Gretta kicked her in the stomach and across the face with one motion. My next move was to get ice from the refrigerator. Gretta looked angrily at me and said, "Clean your shit up!"

I knew then that I couldn't stay with her because on one of my low energy days she could kick my ass. I refused to be controlled by any woman but that day I cleaned my shit up in a hurry.

CHAPTER 20

STRANGE HAPPENINGS

Chinadoll's younger brother came by to see me and was the bearer of bad news. With hurt displayed all over his face he told me that Chinadoll was pregnant. That didn't surprise me but I must admit that I was a little hurt myself. After all, I'd spent almost three years loving and protecting her from that very thing. My vision for us was to have the total forest to enjoy for a lifetime and not just the front row of trees to view; to achieve that I knew that both our careers were a necessity. Having a baby could wait. Be as it may she was pregnant and life had to go on. I asked if she was getting married. He said he didn't know but his father was furious.

Though I wasn't angry, that news cemented the fact that I would not be a part of her life. I would never take her back after she had another man's baby.

***

Summer was just about over and a marvelous one it was. I would be leaving for school in a few weeks but before I went there was this red bone I had to knock off. She was a tiny, fine thing and had been buzzing around trying to give me that ass for a while. She arranged for me to come to her house one morning after her mom left for work. I arrived ready to work, and for three hours I spanked that thing every way possible. I put her on the edge of the sink and watched her cum drip down the drain. Still deep inside her I lifted her tiny, tight ass up and walked around the room playing horsey. I came so good and powerful I blew her off the dick. There's something to be said about small honeys.

The next day I was itching like a motherfucker to the point that I was about to scratch a hole in my ass. Later that afternoon while telling one of my partners what happened, he started laughing.

"What the hell are you laughing about?" I said, still scratching while waiting for his response.

"She gave me the crabs too."

"Why didn't you tell me the bitch had crabs?"

"I didn't know you were trying to fuck her!"

"But you know we keep each other informed about the unclean bitches."

"You right. But shave your hair and get some Blue Star ointment," he advised.

"By the time I finish scratching there won't be anything to shave. I'm going after her ass as soon as I get this itch off me," I said angrily.

"I don't know why, that's not going to get rid of them crabs. You begged her for the pussy and got just what you wanted, just like I did."

"Fuck you. Who are you, a fucking social worker?"

Oh well, when you lie down with dogs you get up with itchy critters, I thought to myself.

All my other ladies were doing just fine, except for the occasional loneliness they experienced when thinking about my departure. I decided to tap Zill's thing one more time before I left. I arrived at her house just after dark to find Zass there. We talked for a few minutes then I suggested that I would leave but Zass indicated that he was leaving. Zill claimed that he came to see his son who was away at her mother's house. Son my ass, he came to make another baby, I thought to myself. I couldn't care less; all I wanted was one last roll in the hay before returning to school. We spent the rest of the night making love as if for the first time. Sex was always great between us. We were like a fine-tuned engine working together with all pistons firing on time and at the right moment. There was no doubt that she loved having sex with me. Even so, I knew her heart belonged to Zass. They had so much history together. A few days after a visit with my general physician my suspicions of what took place between Zill and Zass prior to my arrival was confirmed. I believe that dirty, rotten, stinking dog Zass had deliberately set me up.

I'd learned so much about life that summer. Life was one big game and everyone was playing in their own right, by their own rules. There was no loyalty except to one's self. The game of love and sex was difficult given the time, energy and craftiness that were required to stay one step ahead of the prey and the competition. My weakness was thinking that my great sexual competitiveness would deliver me from the evils of women, making them loyal on the basis of guaranteed good sex rather than a committed, long-term relationship. As I thought about all the love and devotion given to Chinadoll, coupled with the promiscuous women in my life, I came to realize that love and commitment were dynamic; revolving around one's own wants and desires. In other words the nature of the beast was to win. Winning satisfied the soul and it didn't matter at whose expense.

I was back on campus to start my junior year. Being back in the fall was always an exciting time. It was football season and the new female crop was out in full bloom.

To my disapointment I arrived and learned that I had no place to live. My apartment, which was reserved prior to the summer, had been rented to a friend of the owner. My roommate, who had attended summer school, had found an efficiency apartment and offered me the couch, at half the rent I might add. I wasn't totally stupid but realized that that was the only deal at the time. He was still going with the same little ugly girl since his freshman year and had no problem screwing her in my presence. They did it like rabbits, real fast with little squeaky noises and in one position. I would put my head under the covers and laugh my ass off. He was about 5'2" and real funny-looking, kinda like a guinea pig; she was about 4'9" and looked just the same.

He had a habit of trying to do everything that I did, I guess in a competitive nature. I was a very good cook so one Saturday I made a pecan pie and let him taste a small piece. It was truly delicious. He just had to make one so I gave him the recipe but refused to show all of my steps. So little man, as we called him, went to the store and purchased all the ingredients. When the bake time had expired he allowed it to cool as instructed. Licking his lips he cut his pie. Knowing what was about to happen I began my fall-out routine. Using a spatula he scooped up a nice big slice and it ran like water. I fell out. He put it back in the oven and cooked it for another hour. The pecans were burned, the pie was one watery mess, and I was a laughing wreck. After dozens of attempts he still couldn't get it right.

After sleeping on the couch for a month a friend offered to let me cat (living illegally in the dorm) in his room. His roommate had dropped out of school leaving a vacant bed. That was much better not to mention free.

Living next door was a real cool dude name Don, who had both arms amputated at the elbow and both legs amputated at the knee. He was funny, and at times wicked, and thought of himself as a lover.

One day while a group of us were on the set, a tall, good-looking stallion walked by. One would have thought she was a model she was so fly. Sitting in his wheelchair Don said to her, "Hey Baby, come here and let me finger fuck you."

I have to say his remark caught me totally by surprise. I couldn't believe that he had the audacity to disrespect such a lovely lady. Don sure knew how to pick them, I thought. The young lady stopped then looked back and said, "It takes two hands to handle the Whopper."

Everyone went berserk as she totally embarrassed him. In retaliation he got down out of the wheelchair, wobbled over to her on nubs and called her every name in the book. She looked down on him, smiled, and then gracefully walked away. At that moment I knew I had to have her.

Don was handicapped but he had heart and didn't take shit from anyone. His biggest handicap was every time someone needed a battery for their car they stole the one off his wheelchair.

One particular weekend a few of the fellows decided to go to the new nightclub. Don's battery had been stolen so we pushed him to the venue. He was feeling a little horny and thought that he could scoop a chick at the club. Everyone was dancing and having fun, even Don was doing his thing in the wheelchair, when two guys got into a fight over a girl and knocked Don over. That made him very angry. After reseating him he was bumped again. The next thing I knew, he came out of the wheelchair with a gun held between his nibs and started firing round after round. People scattered like roaches when the lights came on. To this day I never discovered how Don shot that gun.

Later that night one of the boys came to my room and said that they saw a guy go into Don's room. Right away I rushed over trying not to miss any of the excitement. We opened the door, which was unlocked, and boy, oh boy! Ripley himself wouldn't have believed the sight. In all my years I've never seen anything that compared to that. Don was on top of the punk who was faced down with a mile of dick up his ass. It was almost as if Don was a yo-yo because with every stroke the punk threw him up in the air and down he came slamming back in that ass. He had nothing to hold on with so there he was flapping like a dishrag blowing in the wind. That was by far the funniest, weirdest thing I'd ever witnessed. When asked why he didn't stop when we came into the room Don said, "He was going to ride that ass until he bucked him off." My association with Mr. Booty-getter ended that night.

***

The Rattlers were playing a game in Atlanta one weekend. Lots of honeys was all I could think about, lots of honeys. Even if I didn't get any sex that weekend I was taking names and numbers to make way for future pussy. I loved out-of-town women because out of sight was out of mind. No one could tell what they couldn't see.

My sister decided to catch the bus to Tallahassee and then ride the rest of the way with me. I decided to take three other homeboys with me to cover the gas.

The game was exciting and the trip was a blast. Everything had gone according to plan. I had a list of possibilities just waiting to be deep dicked.

Getting back that Sunday night I took my sister to the bus station to catch her transportation home. The bus left at

11 p.m., after which I headed back to campus.

A few blocks from the bus station one of the guys informed me that he had stolen a tape case full of 8-track tapes. I was furious because stealing wasn't my thing. Upon arriving at the dorm I informed the thief never to perform such an act while in my car. Then I really got pissed off when he didn't have his share of the money. Six dollars was a lot of money and I made it clear that I wanted it.

A few weeks later I had no gas and no money. No gas and no money equaled no new pussy, a terrible position to be in. My only option was to sell some of the stolen tapes. I went by his room and took the case full of tapes. The tapes were all country western so before going to work at the library I went into the white section of town to sell them. I sold two at the gas station for three dollars each and used that money for gas.

I decided to make one more stop to try and get food money. Pulling into another gas station I readily noticed a cowboy attendant wearing boots and a 10-gallon hat. I just knew that I had a sale. I could taste the Whopper with fries and a Coke. I asked the cowboy gent if he wanted to buy some tapes.

"What you got?" he asked.

"Some country western with good old Charlie Pride," I answered back. White folks love Charlie Pride, I was thinking.

"You betcha," he said. "Wait and let me get some money from my boss and I'll buy them all!" he shouted.

"No problem," I replied.

In less than a minute the whole station was surrounded by sheriff cars. Would you believe the tapes belonged to the cowboy? Out of ninety thousand people in

Tallahassee I tried to sell the tapes to the fucking owner. What rotten fucking luck!

Out of the cars they came, guns cocked and aimed at my black ass. I immediately put both hands in the air then spread my legs and pleaded with them rednecks not to shoot.

"I ought to blow your goddamn head off!" hollered one of them. "Do you hear me, boy?"

"Yes sir, boss! I hear you loud and clear. As long as you have that .45 pointed at my head, I promise to hear every word and do anything you say."

Well, they put me in handcuffs, impounded my car and off to jail I went. They booked me and put me under a $1,000.00 bond. I used my one phone privilege to call the one person I didn't want to call but the only person I knew would get me out, Mom.

Her first question would be, "Did you steal the tapes?" If I said yes my ass would sit until Jesus came. Since I didn't, I was home free. Everything went just as I'd thought, except she didn't have the $100.00 on hand to bail me out. I talked the jailers into letting me make a second phone call then a third. No one I called seemed to have money so for the next ten hours I waited without hearing my name called. It was about 10 p.m when the head jailer came in and in a southern, redneck tone said, "Well boy, we're gonna have to lock you down."

"I ain't your boy and you ain't putting me in no cell. My bondsman is coming to get me," I retaliated.

Seeing my refusal to cooperate he turned and shouted to someone in the back, "Billy Bob and Jimbo, you boys come on out here!" I heard the steel door open and out came the biggest, ugliest, meanest looking white boys I had ever seen.

"Ya'll lock this boy up," he said.

"Don't touch me, I can walk by myself!" I said, and then hurriedly got my ass in the cell.

If being locked down wasn't bad enough, try it when the only television program you are allowed to watch is *Hee Haw*, a dumb hillbilly program about stupid folks. That was my first time in jail and all I could think about was somebody trying to get my booty. I was willing to die before I let such a thing happen and was prepared to fight to the death. Luckily for me I was the biggest thing in the cell block and the guy in the bunk next to me was from school. He was in for forging checks so I suggested that if he was released first he should do his best work to get my black ass out of there.

About 11:30 p.m. my name was called. My ass had been sprung. Thank God for Mom, I prayed. In the end I was given three years probation after dealing with a crooked lawyer, a crooked district attorney, who was the lawyer's brother-in-law, and a crooked judge, all of whom shared the money.

A few days after being released from jail I met the stallion Don had insulted. I introduced myself then acknowledged that I was a witness to Don's assault on her a few weeks earlier and expressed how wrong and juvenile he had been.

As sophisticated as she was, I felt my best approach was to show some compassion; after all, I didn't know whether or not she had observed me at the scene and felt that I was a part of it. That way I would erase all doubts. She told me that her name was Angie and she lived in the new dorm just across from where I was staying. We sat and talked for a long while in the courtyard that separated the men's and women's dorms. She revealed that she was involved in a rocky relationship with a Kappa and was uncertain as to its future. Her being in a relationship didn't faze me at all. The fact that she was with the #1 Kappa on campus made it more exciting. There was nothing better that I'd like than to clip his wings, which I knew would surely happen. I was never one for pledging or group affiliations.

I made it very clear that I would love to spend time with her without causing any problems, knowing all the time that was just what I wanted to do. I asked if I could see her the following evening and she said yes. Another notch on the gun, I thought.

I picked her up just after dark to keep from being seen. Having the entire night planned out in advance I drove to the stadium and parked. It was pitch black dark. There were absolutely no lights, not even a star bright. I had all night so there was no need for me to rush it. We discussed many different subjects during which I complimented her smile, her lovely appearance, and anything else I thought would get me between her thighs.

After a while I sensed that she had become more comfortable with me so I started stroking her hair just above the forehead and around the ears. I slowly slid my fingers very lightly down her arms, barely touching her. She shivered as goosebumps appeared all over her body. She was done and I knew it! I kissed her hard as she grabbed the bulge in my pants.

Pulling away from my kiss with her mouth still open she mumbled, "Oh, my God!" while still holding her new joystick. Continuing to kiss me she took my hand and moved it toward the wetness of her inner thighs. I refused to let her go there. I wanted to gain the upper hand, making her want me by not giving her what she desired. She was mine and I knew it. I had her body so hot you could stick a cigar in her pussy and light that motherfucker without puffing.

I backed off, expressing that she was far more important to me than sex. At that point her heart, mind, body and soul were completely and totally fucked up. As for me there was no way I was going to make love to that fine specimen of a woman in the back seat of a car. I had the plan, the time, the place, and now I had the bitch. Destiny was mine!

I deliberately ignored her for the next few days because I wanted her to miss me bad. Upon seeing me a few days after our little rendezvous she rushed over like a wench to the master.

"Why haven't I seen you?" she asked.

"You said there was someone else so I didn't want to crowd your space. Besides, I was protecting my heart," the fox in me replied.

"Protect your heart! Well who's going to protect mine?" she asked matter-of-factly.

"I will," I said, staring softly in her eyes.

She smiled then gave me a soft kiss and a caring hug. Boy, what was it going to be like when I spanked that monkey? I thought.

Just as we turned to leave we saw her used-to-be boyfriend watching us with a nasty look on his face; the kind of look a nigga has when he's about to kill. He must have thought that as the #1 Kappa on campus this should not be happening to him. Well, homeboy, just in case you didn't know how, and or why, it didn't matter once it was done. She indicated the need to talk to him and end it properly. I agreed but was a bit concerned that he might get violent; however, she didn't appear worried.

"See you later," I said, and then walked away.

The dean of men found out that I was living in the dorm illegally and threatened my roommate. I had no intention of getting him in further trouble so I moved out. An older homeboy working on campus allowed me to share his apartment for a fair monthly fee. That was much better and definitely more private than living in the dorm. Angie was with me when I moved in so I introduced her to my roommate. Later that night after I took her back to her room my homeboy alleged that he had seen her around campus and that she was an upstanding young lady. Yeah, that weekend she was going to have my upstanding dick all up in her lying-down ass, I thought.

***

The weekend arrived and it was Angie's time to be sanctified. She showed up on time just as my roommate went out for the night. Show time! The ice had already been broken so there was no need for hesitation or caution. Holding her hand, I led her straight to my bedroom. I put on some jazz, stripped her naked and got busy. There was something to be said about good-looking, long-legged women. When I got her to the point of a heat explosion I decided to tease a bit. I pulled away as I had done a few days earlier, stating that she was much too respectable to have sex with. That's when the animal in her showed up.

Pretty lady wrapped them long legs around me one-and-a-half times, snatched me into her and buried my dick so deep that she was sucking while I was fucking. She had me clutched tighter than an octopus on a shellfish. If it was a short night I would have lost, but the night was long and my wind was strong.

Shortly after I regained my composure she started speaking in tongue as her pussy was ready to explode. I grabbed the headboard with both hands while giving long, deep strokes. Her legs unraveled as she lifted them high over her head. I raised on my toes gaining traction as she screamed, "Hurt me you motherfucker, who's dick is this?"

I was in control now, I thought as I was steadily laying pipe to her ass. I could feel the wet warmth of her cum surrounding my penis as the pressure of her release blew my dick out. Looking down I thought she had Niagara Falls in her pussy. That bitch could have filled up a 16 oz. Coke bottle. She indicated that she was thirsty and requested something to drink. I was thinking, no shit, as I got up to get a jug of jungle punch, otherwise known as ice water.

Upon my return I noticed that her cum had flooded the entire center of the bed. I moved her to a dry spot and fucked her ass until my nuts went flat. What a night! The tune of *ain't no pussy like the long-legged pussy*, kept playing over and over in my head. The next time I was going to sing it while I was fucking her.

A couple of days later I picked her up and went for a drive. Somehow I knew that we'd end up in my favorite spot down by the stadium. I would have preferred to take her to the crib but my roommate was at home with friends. I parked in my usual dark spot. Conversation was always good between us since she was a highly intelligent young lady, a born and bred New Yorker with a style and grace indicative of one from the Big Apple. I quickly got into the rhythm of touching all the right spots. We both loved the feeling that we got from each other but this time she decided to take the challenge of making me cum orally. In a previous discussion I had mentioned that even though I'd had my hambone sucked on many occasions no one had ever made me cum. She had a hard time understanding why, and I had a hard time understanding why she couldn't understand why.

Was she the suck-dick expert? I wondered. "How many cocks had she had in her mouth?" I asked myself. I could see that kissing was about to become a problem. Where I came from oral sex for men was taboo, or so I thought. Before I could lose focus she had my dick's head in her mouth. Either she had done this before or she had a lot of practice sucking on candy canes, I thought; be as it may, that bitch was good. Cumming orally had to be a mental thing because she was sucking air through my ass hole and I still hadn't come. After what seemed like forever my body went into spasms. My booty tightened up at the same time my penis's head started throbbing. My pump had been primed. I shot off so hard I put a jut on the back of her head.

"Oh, Baby, no one can make me cum sucking my dick like you did!"

"Did you like it?"

"I love it. Goddamn I love it."

I've come to believe that everyone has a specialty, something they do better than anyone else and Angie's was blow jobs. She was now a permanent employee. Anytime she wanted to work on my dick she was more than welcome. The bitch could suck out the sweet inside of a lollipop without disturbing the outer candy. I mean homegirl could pull fresh air from the outside through the ass hole. I didn't care whose dick she had sucked in the past, if I had to kiss to get it, so be it! Thank God for mouthwash!

We visited that spot many times more over the next few months. Angie made sucking my dick a ritual. A word of wisdom to all wise women, "If you want to keep your man in bed, stay on that head."

After a couple of months of living with my roommate I started wondering about his sexual preference. He spent more time watching my dick than his own. He never went out on dates with women or had any over. Even though he had never made a pass at me I just had that funny feeling.

He seemed a little strange so I decided to look for another place. In just a few days I found a one-bedroom efficiency within my budget. Without hesitation I put my box spring and mattress on top of my car and off I went.

I had two young fine things for neighbors and it was my nature to chase the best of the two. My motto was, "If you can't get the best, go for the rest." But right now I was going for the better of the two. Shortly after moving in I invited the best-looking one over for dinner. It was the middle of December 1970 and very cold. I decided to prepare a dish my daddy called dad-had, made by boiling onions and stew beef—you may know it as cubed beef— until tender, then adding tomatoes, corn and okra with a side order of corn bread, and pecan pie for dessert. She fell in love with the dad-had but gave up the pussy after eating my pecan pie. A big slice of pecan pie would guarantee all night in the pussy. She was no stranger to fucking and I was right at home baking my ass off.

Whenever I wasn't playing in someone else's pussy I would call her and ask if she wanted a piece of pecan pie because I surely wanted a piece of that pussy. I shaked and baked until I went home for the Christmas holidays.

CHAPTER 21

LUST'S DIVIDENDS

Even though the fun time of the year had ended (football season) I couldn't wait to get back to school. I had about five or six little honeys on the string and I was chasing this big-boned stallion from Quincy, Florida. I couldn't wait to ride her ass like a cowboy riding a bronco bull and make her buck me while she fucked me. After a few weeks of teasing conversation she gave in. I don't know if it was due to my constant begging or she just had to have me, but what a rodeo.

Three days later I made a trip to the clinic. The doctor gave me a week's supply of sulfur pills. After a few days my ass began to itch then I noticed that my genitals were getting raw. Before I knew it my whole body was one big rash. I decided to drive home and see my family doctor to discover that I was allergic to sulfur. Bad pussy and bad medicine equate to one sick puppy. Upon returning to school I read that stink-ho her rights.

After a few days I was like brand new and horny as hell after almost two weeks with no sex. Subsequent to my mishap I made a conscious decision to play within the inner circle of women I'd created for the remainder of the grading period. In other words I was going to chill on recruiting unless someone just happened to fall in my lap. Angie remained at the top of my list with pecan pussy a close second—she could fuck the nuts from the pie without disturbing the jelly.

It was spring break and just about everyone including me was going home. I was looking forward to a change of scenery after a long, cold winter in Tallahassee, which at times felt like the coldest place on earth.

The day after I arrived home I decided to go visit teachers and friends at my old high school. Just as I was about to leave my eyes focused on a very cute cheerleader. She had a big, beautiful afro with an attractive smile underneath like decoration. She was young and tender but plump in all the right places. But with all her beauty it was the dimples in her thighs that got my goose. My adrenalin quickly went into overdrive. I wanted her. I asked a friend who she was and if she had a boyfriend. He broke her down like he was her biographer.

I went to work as he called her over to make the introduction. I acted as if I had no knowledge of her, requesting the same information I'd already received. That was one of the ways I used to check honesty and character. Upon my request she told me her name was Ny'lora then gave me her phone number.

Heaven had opened up its doors and shined on me one more time, I smiled to myself. I remember that was the same spot I had first met Chinadoll almost four years prior. Later that evening Ny'lora and I talked on the phone and she agreed to me visiting her on Saturday night.

I arrived at her house just after dark. She greeted me with the same bubbling smile that lit up her face a few days earlier. With her heart palpitating rapidly I could tell that she was surprised to see me. Later she revealed that she didn't think I would show up.

Once inside the house she introduced me to her mother and other family members. After meeting her sister I quickly remembered that she was one of the chicks who was supposed to have played hooky with me about six years earlier.

The tantalizing look on her sister's face told me that she was much aware of who I was. Back then Ny'lora had talked badly about me to her sister, and perhaps that was the main reason her sister and I had not gotten together. I was thinking that strangely enough, either Ny'lora just didn't remember all of that from back then, or she just chose to conveniently forget. At that moment I figured there was little chance of me getting any action from that household but I decided to stay and play the hand I was dealt. Despite early tension the night ended quite well with a passionate kiss and hug.

I called Ny'lora the following day before returning to school. I wanted her to know that I was very interested in her. Mainly I wanted to know if her sister had created any problems for me by refreshing her memory. I didn't sense any tension as we talked. I could tell that she was interested in me as she expressed a mild sadness about me leaving so soon. I assured her that I would be in touch.

As soon as I got back to school I made a pecan pie, and well...you know the rest. I quickly got back into my usual routine of hitting here and there making sure everyone in my stable was satisfied. I invested a phone call to Ny'lora every four or five days hoping for dividends in the near future.

Two weeks had passed since I had last seen my new high school sweetheart. I decided to go home and test the water as we say. Ny'lora had a large family who lived in a very small house. Everywhere I turned I had four eyes watching me. About 12:30 a.m. I had a stroke of luck. Everyone including her mother went to bed. We had waited long and patiently for that moment. Serious kissing with heavy petting followed. We generated unbelievable passion. If someone had sprinkled water on us we would have sizzled like a frying pan on a hot stove. Suddenly a voice came from the room, "Ny'lora, I know that boy ain't still in my house." At that moment me and my stiff dick hit the door without even getting a good-night kiss. As I drove home, I thought, she truly has pizzazz.

The next day I was shocked when she asked me if I would escort her to the senior prom. I immediately thought that being seen at the prom was the same as being branded. Everybody would know who I was seeing. I had always had a problem with being out in the open; it lessened my chances for future prey. But I knew that if I didn't take her to the prom I would not get the rose. And the rose I did want. So guess what?

There I was back home the day before the big event ordering a carnation and getting fitted for a black tuxedo. Ny'lora had given me her word that after the prom and the class party we would spend the rest of the night together. That alone guaranteed that her date would show up on time for her senior prom. I'd made plans with my baby sister to have her apartment for the night. She even allowed us to sleep in her bed. What a caring, darling sister!

The prom and the after party were quite nice and I felt very comfortable being amongst the younger crowd. That was her night but now it was Pookey's time and shine I would. I love having all night, I thought. I can be long and slow, repeatedly.

We arrived at my sister's house about 2 a.m. I turned on the light in the stairway and we went immediately upstairs to the bedroom. There was an innocence about her that caused me to be gentle. Perhaps that was a part of her youthfulness, which I came to admire.

"Are you OK with this?" I asked.

"Yes, I'm OK."

"Are you sure?"

"Sure I'm sure!"

"Because I don't want you to do this if you're not ready."

"Thanks for caring about my feelings but I want to share this part of me with you."

I kissed her passionately as we slowly undressed. I introduced her to a new playground as our lustful bodies met with hot passion. Somehow she touched me unlike the women whose great sex I came to appreciate and enjoy. Perhaps this was the one, I thought for a brief moment before reality kicked in; I knew my sexuality belonged to no one but to everyone of my interest.

I decided to attend summer school to ensure on-time graduation in June of 1972. It was very hot and appeared to be the year of the gnats—they were everywhere. Very few if any activities took place during that term, which made things very boring.

There was a glitter in the midst of boredom. My sweet princess, missing me as much as I missed her, caught the Greyhound bus to Tallahassee for a weekend with her new and exciting love. I had worked her good so I wasn't surprised that she rode "the dog" eight hours to be mounted. We checked into the Travelodge motel just after 6 p.m. Friday. For dinner I took her to the Sizzler Steak House. That was heaven for her because all I ever saw her family eat was red beans and rice; never saw any meat. I guess it was the beans that plumped her ass up—she was nice and firm.

Once back in the room we wasted no time showing each other love. Other than going out for an occasional meal, all of our time was spent making love. She was like my favorite dessert and I had a craving for her body.

The weekend went quickly. I had nourished and loved her beyond her greatest expectation. She wept as she boarded the bus for the long ride home. After a loving hug and kiss I promised to be home in a couple of weeks.

The campus was almost like a ghost town as very few students, especially women, had attended summer school. Perhaps that was the reason I missed Ny'lora so immensely. Not a day went by that I didn't drift into obsession.

Finally the misery was lifted as summer school ended. I had three weeks home with my baby and nothing to do but sex her up. We spent a lot of time going to dinner and to the movies. She often asked me to have dinner at her house but all I could think about was red beans and rice with no meat. I made it a point to eat before I got to her abode so I could legitimately say I had eaten whenever she asked me to dine with them. Besides, the way I saw her sisters and brothers fight over the last piece of bread there was just no way.

One morning while looking out my back door I observed a young lady walking up the sidewalk who I'd known from junior high school. I sprinted from the house to meet and greet her. I was astonished at the fact that she knew me right away—including my name. Realizing I didn't remember her name she quickly introduced herself as Dedra, and further revealed that she and her family had just moved into the project around the corner. A 30-second walk, I thought as I smiled mischievously. And I'd be damn if she wasn't as pretty as she had been then; black as coal with pearl-white teeth and skin soft as velvet. All I knew was that I was hot for her in junior high and I was burning up for her now. I realized then that the growl in me was so deep that it was impossible for the dog to go away. I was panting with lust in my heart as she walked away with a smile of approval. I imagined how delightful it would be. God is a good God even when you don't know Him, I testified.

I never believed in wasting precious time so the next day I showed up at Dedra's house—clean. There were some very nosey neighbors living in front of her apartment so I went to the back door. It was about noon and she was home alone. Her mother and brother were at work and neither would be home before 4 p.m. We talked casually for about one half hour. She told me that she was married and her husband was overseas; then in the same breath told me how much she had always admired me.

I was thinking, I hadn't seen her in probably seven years so how could she have been admiring me? But the reality of a hard dick quickly let me know that I didn't give a damn. She was very laid-back, making it easy for us to be comfortable with each other. She responded with goose pimples as I gently stroked her arms. Her passion increased beyond my expectation as I kissed her neck and ear. I was in total control and knew it. I took her hand, leading her upstairs to the bedroom. While undressing her I caressed her body, kissed her softly, and brought her to full rapture. As I entered her, the tightness of her vagina told me how much in need she was of some loving. Her husband was away and she was starving for dick. I stroked her slowly with deep, smooth rhythm. Perspiration developed rapidly over her body with her pupils disappearing at times.

"Oh, God I want to cum!" she screamed.

As our bodies reached full ecstasy her eyes disappeared. Her entire body trembled like she was having a seizure. All of a sudden she became lifeless, as if in a coma. After fifteen minutes of talking and praying I got no response.

"Oh, God, please don't let her be dead. Lord I'll be good if you just let her come back to life," I prayed. "Oh, shit! I've been a bad boy and He's not going to answer me," I said to myself.

It was about 3:45 p.m. and her mom would be home in fifteen minutes. I rushed to the bathroom where I found some alcohol in the medicine cabinet. Wetting a towel with cold water I began wiping down her body. With my finger I dropped a small amount of the alcohol in her nostrils, but still no response.

"God, what am I going to do? I don't want to go to jail," I continued to pray.

Wetting the towel again I squeezed water over her face and body then filled the cap from the bottle and started pouring alcohol up her nose. Finally at 3:59 p.m. she coughed. That cough felt better than the nut I had just had, I thought. She was cognizant but looking as if she had just shot heroin up her vein. I ran to the front window to see if her mom was in view. No mom in sight! What a blessing. After wiping her body down I helped her get dressed as she slowly came around. I had just put one foot in my trousers when I heard a knock at the front door. Good, she had locked the screen door at my request. At that point she was on her own. My ass hit the back door with shoes and shirt in hand; I was running faster than a jackrabbit.

The next day I went over to find out how her mother had reacted to the screen door being locked. Dedra said, "I told her I had fallen asleep and didn't hear her knocking."

Just a harmless little white lie, I thought. She smiled with a joyful expression when I commented on how sexually wonderful she was. During our conversation she told me that her husband had never come close to making her feel as good as I did, not to mention that he had never made her cum.

"I've never felt anything like that. The sensation was so intense. I must have lost consciousness!"

"Yes, you did. You transcended from this world to a more blissful place. I took you there," I said, smiling with confidence.

"Please don't let my being married interfere in anyway with our relationship. My heart, body and all that you desire of me is yours," she promised.

"Trust me, I've already forgotten that you are married," I said, as she kissed me passionately.

"Let's go upstairs," she suggested.

Knowing that I had to give Ny'lora some loving that night I quickly responded, "Baby, I want the relationship to be more than just sex so let's talk and learn to appreciate being with each other." After a smooch she thanked me for being so caring. I knew I had her head all fucked up and I owned her body. She smiled as she rested her head on my shoulder. Lord, I was thinking, why has thou blessed me so?

Ny'lora and I agreed that when it was time for me to return to school she would go back with me. She had graduated from high school a few months earlier and decided that she wanted to spend the rest of her life with me. I felt that living together would be a good thing. It would allow me to focus more on my studies by keeping me out of the streets. Besides, there's nothing better than instant pussy.

Well, I broke the news to my mother and she was pissed. With tears in her eyes and sadness in her voice she pleaded her case, stressing that the added responsibility would force me to get a job leaving little time for studying. Education was very important to my mom. She wanted nothing to interfere with me getting my degree on time. I assured her that I would surely graduate on time and that I most definitely was not going to work. I told her the agreement was that Ny'lora would work, buy the food, and take care of the house while I went to school.

Ny'lora told her mom the news later that evening and she became totally hostile. I felt no pain as she threatened to kill me if I attempted to take her daughter away from home. Understanding that I was not her favorite person I sat quietly trying not to agitate the situation further. However, I could understand her mom's anger. Ny'lora did all the cooking and took care of the house and her siblings.

Sunday, the day of departure, came quickly. Ny'lora had packed the night before so when I arrived at her house the only thing to do was load the car. Her mom begged and pleaded with her not to leave.

"Mama I love him and I'm going," she said.

Her mother cried frantically then proceeded to call me every name imaginable. As I loaded her stuff in the car her mom rushed outside, picked up a red brick and shouted, "I'll bust a hole in your goddamn head if you take my daughter!"

Believing that she would I moved around to the driver's side and got in. After Ny'lora entered, her mom got in front of the car then drew back the brick and said, "I'll break this goddamn window."

At that point I'd had enough of being cursed and threatened so I got out of the car and said, "If you bust my window I'm going to bust your ass!"

Hurting deeply she dropped the brick and walked toward the house without looking back, not even for a glance.

We arrived in Tallahassee before dark to a trailer home my neighbor and friend had rented for me. It was a two-bedroom split plan with living, dining, kitchen and one bathroom; quite spacious and in great shape. After unpacking we went to get some food and household items. Right away she started whipping our new home into shape with a woman's touch. As I watched her at work I thought, this was the first time I had any woman in my house with no thoughts of letting her go. I was in for the long haul but was the dog in me?

We retired to bed just before midnight. I sat staring at her gorgeous body as she lay naked beside me. Her 5'4," 115-pound frame with those dimples in her thighs made me feel like I was in hog heaven. I caressed her all over with extreme gentleness until her body quivered. I kissed her passionately as I stroked the head beneath her soft, fluffed-out afro.

As I sucked her breasts while playing with her clitoris she was brought to tears of joy. She begged me to enter, but from experience I knew what time was the right time. Kissing her softly and touching all the hot spots I'd become friends with made the bright-red cherry between her legs stand up. The little monkey in the boat was now ready; dripping juices helped lubricate her tight cunt as I entered my dick's head. I stroked her carefully, not to cause pain but pure pleasure. When the little monkey reached out and grabbed all of the head I slowly eased the shaft deep inside; so deep, I ran out of pussy. If I went any deeper I'd be fucking her in the ass hole at the same time. She was tight.

Her vagina fit my dick like a glove, I thought. Her rhythm increased as she cried while digging her nails in my back.

"I'm cumming!" she howled. "Oh, my God, I'm cumming!"

The friction was so great and the feeling intense that I either had to cum in it or get out of it, I thought. I decided to cum when she came. After what I had just put on her she wouldn't have energy to cum again. Ah, the night was a most enjoyable one. I wondered if what we felt would last forever.

It didn't take my baby long to find a job as a waitress. She worked days, which gave us the opportunity to spend evenings together. I studied every night while she prepared dinner, and sometimes after she fell asleep. If nothing else her presence guaranteed that I would graduate on time. My grades had improved proportionately with my study habits. Things were good. We were having lots of fun together and the sex was terrific and steady. I had to have sex every night.

Even when she was too tired to throw it back I wanted it. I would tell her to turn her back to me, toot her ass out and just wiggle with the dick. After two months of straight pussy, some mornings I would be too tired to get out of bed so I would roll to the floor and crawl to the shower to become invigorated. The good thing about me was my dick didn't need much rest. I was a true dicksman and proud of it.

CHAPTER 22

UNBELIEVABLE

It was Homecoming weekend. My sister was coming for the game, and guess what? Dedra was coming with her. They planned to arrive Thursday night in order to enjoy the entire weekend. And guess what else? We'd all be living under the same roof. No outs, the bases were loaded and I was up to bat getting ready to grandslam their asses. Ny'lora had to work Friday. Great, I thought, we needed the money. About 8:30 that morning I told my sister that I was going to show Dedra around the town while she got some rest. I took Dedra straight to the Roadway Inn Hotel.

After making her pay for the room I jumped head over heels into that pussy. She was desperate for dick, not having any since I left. I fucked her ass into a new beginning; once again leaving her comatose. She had promised that her heart, body and all that I desired was mine, and on that day she was not lying.

Dedra and I left the hotel in time for me to take her to my house before picking up Ny'lora. When we arrived my sister was pissed, saying that Ny'lora had been calling all day.

"Oh, shit!" I said. "What did you tell her?"

"I told her the truth."

"What truth?" I asked.

"The truth that you and Dedra had been gone all day," she responded.

"I'm fucked and Dedra is dead," I said silently.

When I arrived at Ny'lora's job she was madder than a pimp with no pussy or should I say, an angry pimp with a broke whore.

"I want to know where the hell you and Dedra have been all day," she inquired. "It don't take all damn day to give somebody a tour, and besides, why didn't you take your sister along?"

"What are you trying to say?" I asked.

"I ain't trying to say shit! I'm saying straight up that if I find out that both of you was at a motel, I'm going to kick her ass into tomorrow," she answered angrily. "I don't like that black bitch anyways and the nerve of that whore; come to my house, eat my food and lay up and fuck you all day...oh, hell no!" she said furiously. "I can't wait to get to the fucking house!" She was heated.

Calmly I said, "Baby, you are upset over nothing. All we did was ride around the town looking at the sites then she offered to treat me to lunch to show appreciation for the extended hospitality. You know that I love you," I said. "But if you are that jealous I just won't be friendly to anyone else, I don't want to cause trouble between us so feel free to interrogate Dedra and do whatever it takes to satisfy yourself, and when you find out that you have made a fool out of yourself, just know that I still love you," I told her, leaning over to give her a kiss. She said nothing, but I knew I had her in the palm of my hand.

When we got home, baby sister had cooked dinner and everything was nice. We stuffed our guts while talking and having a good time. Ny'lora didn't seem to be mad anymore as she displayed that cheerful smile. After overeating and drinking, I politely mentioned that I had to go to the bathroom.

Without hesitation Dedra said, "I have to go too." Then all hell broke loose. Ny'lora jumped up and said, "You better piss outside or in a goddamn cup because you damn sure ain't going to the toilet with him. You and him had been gone all day and I want to know what the fuck you both were doing?" she shouted.

Before Dedra could answer my sister yelled out, "I got to go to the bathroom myself but I guess I better piss outside!"

Everyone burst into laughter. That seemed to defuse a potentionally hostile situation. Dedra apologized, assuring her that she meant no disrespect for keeping me all day. I was smiling because all was good.

**

Ike and Tina Turner were coming to town. My neighbor Mavel, who was screwing the administrator over special activities, got Ny'lora and I front-row tickets to the show. I had never bought their music but I would never give up the opportunity to sit front row, dead center between Tina's legs. The show went on. The stage was about four feet higher than our seats. Tina came out in this little skimpy outfit cut so close I could see the edge of her hairs. My dick jumped hard without hesitation. I think Tina picked that night to fuck with me. All night long she flaunted her thing right in front of my face. My focus was on one spot as I was mesmerized by her every move.

I wore the hard all the way home. I didn't have Tina but I had a Mrs. Turner look-a-like...just as fine and better looking. As soon as we walked into the house I said to my baby, "Go'n to the room girl cause I'm fixin' to give you some of that good good loving."

As I was undressing I went to the bathroom to take a leak, a kind of ritual for me; urinating before sex seemed to yield more control to propel longevity. With my honey lying amongst the sheets of the dimly lit room my throbbing dickhead had me believing that Tina Turner was in my bed. I went to work on it and after awhile it didn't make any difference who I was banging because all of me was happy.

Just for the record, ain't no sense in all you quick cum, limp-dick readers thinking that all you have to do is take a piss and you can fuck all night. It ain't going to happen. Stamina is built up over time as you push your body to the limit, then you can consider yourself a dicksman.

A few weeks later I observed my baby vomiting during the early morning hours. At first I thought it was the flu since it had been very cold. But when it persisted beyond the normal recovery time I began to ask questions.

"Are you pregnant?"

She cheerfully said yes without hesitation and with a big smile on her face.

"How could you be pregnant when you are on the pill?"

"Well, Baby," she said, "I forgot to take them a few days."

"How many days?" I quizzed her.

"About thirty."

With no job, no money, and no degree I blew my stack. "Thirty days ain't no damn forgot...that's a fucking conspiracy! I can't take care of my black ass so how in the world am I going to take care of a baby?" I asked.

Starting to cry she looked sadly at me then said, "I didn't do it by myself!"

"No you sure as hell didn't, I should have been shoving them pills up your ass instead of my dick," I screamed.

Sadness fell upon her like darkness after a beautiful day. She walked away sobbing. As I left the house I had the feeling of a caged animal rather than a carefree student. I'd been trapped. "I should have listened to my mama...but oh, no...I just had to have my nightly dose of instant pussy," I said while arguing with myself.

Looking down at my dick, I said, "It's your fault, if you weren't so quick to rise and stick, none of this shit would have happened. Fuck you dickhead!"

After two hours of riding and thinking about the whole equation I decided to return home. Calculating the due date I realized that the baby would be born in June. Perhaps things wouldn't be so bad. At least I'd have a degree and maybe a job by the time the baby came, I thought.

Entering the house I could hear Ny'lora crying in the bedroom. I hesitated a moment trying to think of the right thing to say even though it was obvious that I was the victim of a masterful plan. I'd been bamboozled and there was nothing I could do. The hunter had been captured by the game. Gathering my composure I committed myself to showing some compassion. She lay partially on her stomach so I positioned myself behind her, holding her gently without saying a word.

Strangely, in the midst of deliberate entrapment her tears made me succumb to the reality of God's miracle. This was my child...my first, I thought. After holding her for what seemed like forever I broke the silence by saying in a reassuring tone, "Baby, don't cry...everything will be all right." Turning her toward me I hugged her firmly and gave her kisses for assurance and encouragement. My cock also found some compassion, in a matter of minutes that same old no good dick that was so quick to rise and stick suddenly caught the mumps. Guess you know the rest!

The fall session had ended. It was the Christmas season and we were on our way home for the holidays. We decided to break the news to our parents during the week of Christmas; after all, who could stay angry during the celebration of Christ's birth?

After I became settled my mother and I sat down for a one-on-one conversation. She was interested in knowing how well my live-in arrangements were, but more concerned about my grades. When I told her that I had a 3.5 GPA for the term she was ecstatic. I assured her that graduation was all but done. At that moment I decided to share the news; I told her that she was going to be a grandmother. Her exuberance dwindled substantially.

"It doesn't surprise me! I knew that thing would eventually get you in trouble," she said. "I won't support ya'll and I don't babysit...I did my time raising ya'll and after you I was done."

I was thinking, after the ass whippings you put on me I don't want you to keep mine anyway!

When Ny'lora told her mom the news she totally flipped. She lashed out at her saying, "I told you that boy was no damn good. I knew he was going to get you pregnant and dump your ass."

I sat there quiet as a mouse as Ny'lora tried to tell her different. Not knowing from whence a brick might come I sat close by the door. That attitude definitely put a damper on my next plan. Ny'lora and I had decided that it would be better if she stayed home for the rest of the school year since she was approaching four months. Rather than ask her mother if she could stay at home I asked good old baby sister for help. As usual she came through like a champ. After a couple of weeks her mom could no longer endure the temptation of her favorite daughter. Ny'lora moved back home and I returned to school.

Shortly after returning to school I rented the spare bedroom to one of my homies named Zee. Zee was highly intellectual and sort of quiet. I charged him almost as much for rent as I was paying for the trailer; that allowed me the opportunity to send money to Ny'lora.

Zee had two main problems. One, he liked being high more than going to class and two, he was completely depressed over a woman who had ripped his guts out. I thought I was bad after Chinadoll dumped me but this boy had a case of extreme blues, which was why he was indulging so frequently, rendering him immobile at class time. Zee was definitely not a ladies man during high school. As a matter of fact he was quite the opposite. The woman who had inflicted the pain was a grade behind me. She was a real slickster and far too much woman for Zee. He was way out of his league.

After learning the identity of the lady I told Zee that he had been blessed and he should thank God for not letting him put a bullet through his head. That's just what would have happened if he had continued with that witch. I thought about how God sometimes steps in and gives us a little pain to save us from a lifetime of misery. She was a lady of the streets and like me; she knew how to pick her victims. I was her huckleberry and pick from my tree she wouldn't dare.

I really felt sorry for Zee because I understood what he felt. It was hard to love someone so deeply who was invisible to your touch—no matter where you are, no matter what you are doing, your every thought is on her. The pain is revolving and a constant reminder of what once was.

She had moved on but his heart lingered on the hope of one day getting her back. It was quite disheartening for me to see him day after day in his room grieving. He did nothing except listen to the lyrics of a song titled, *Hope she'll be happier* by Bill Withers.

Maybe the lateness of the hour
Make me seem bluer than I am
But in my heart there is shower
Hope she will be happier with him

Over and over, day after day, night after night he played that record. The real sad part about it was that she had left him over a year ago. He could not shake it and I couldn't help him.

During one of my parties pussy was flowing so freely I tried pouring some on him but homeboy acted like seducing women had gone out of style. With tears surfing down his face all he could say was, "I love her and I can't live without her!"

After another month of that mourning and fucking groaning I finally said, "Go ahead and kill your damn self, just don't do it in my trailer. Either get the mourning out of your ass or get your ass out of here. I was fucked up just like you but it took new pussy to get rid of old pain."

I guess he realized that I wasn't dealing with the self-pity bullshit so he began to show signs of life—he brushed his teeth in the morning and even though he still wasn't getting any pussy, he had at least stopped singing the blues 24-7.

One afternoon during a routine visit to the mathematics department, my professor asked me to teach a freshman class the following day. Naturally I agreed to his request. I dressed the part by putting on my best suit; I was cleaner than a sweet-dick dog. Class was going well until this fly honey decided to be a heckler; I guessed she thought that since I was the substitute teacher she could handle me. Boy, was she wrong. I quickly calmed her down by exposing how little she knew about mathematics.

After class I asked to speak with her, basically to apologize for embarrassing her. Quickly I learned that her motive was to draw my attention to her and that the heckling was merely a ploy. I must admit that she was fine as old wine with her high-yellow self. I remember her wearing brown leather boots, a blouse tied in front, and tightly fitted hot pants. What she didn't know was that my dick smiled from ear to ear when I saw her melon-shaped ass walk in. I had to restrain myself even though I was drooling. God knows she was slamming.

During our brief conversation I managed to get all the pertinent information. Her name was Gem and she lived in the freshman dorm; I wasted no time making her acquaintance. Gem was a lot of fun and a pleasure to be around. I started to care for her a lot but I had one problem, Ny'lora was back home pregnant.

My heart wouldn't let me dog Gem so I took things slowly. She was a virgin and green to the ways of the world. She was vulnerable but I vowed to protect her. She was the woman every man wanted to take home to meet Mama.

After we had been together for a few weeks I allowed her to come to one of my usual weekend parties. By now all the fellows knew she was my lady, which meant hands off. Before the party some of the guys, including me and Jet, would chip-in and buy a case of Boonesfarm Strawberry Hill wine. Anonymously, Jet and I would pour out about one cup of the wine then fill the bottles with Everclear (190-proof grain alcohol). My personal bartender had been instructed to give the spiked wine to all the ladies and the men outside the clique. Gem and Jet's lady were the only chicks who didn't drink the magic potion. At about midnight the members only had a free-for-all as the females succumbed to the powers of the fire water; "Ain't no pussy like the intoxicated pussy," was our slogan.

During spring break I arranged to spend two nights and three days in Daytona Beach with Gem; she had gotten permission to spend a couple of days with her best friend. I took my friend Mo to acquaint and keep Gem's friend company.

When we arrived the ladies were waiting at a predetermined location. Before going out we rented adjoining rooms at the Holiday Inn.

It was early in the afternoon so we decided to explore the boardwalk on the beach. We had a great time enjoying the beach and eating.

We returned to the hotel just after dark. Gem and I went immediately to our room to spend some quality time away from the others. Mo was in agreement with the game plan and felt that would provide him the opportunity to get intimate with Gem's friend. Shortly after entering the room, Gem's friend knocked on the door wanting to know what we were doing.

"We are cleaning fish!" I yelled out.

"What kind of fish?"

"The kind that don't want to be bothered!"

After several more knocks we opened the divider door and chatted for a short while. Gem and I expressed that we would like to be alone and suggested that she and Mo do the same. Up until that point I'd never made love to Gem. In the past she appeared to be apprehensive about sex; perhaps it was her deep spiritual upbringing or maybe she was fearful of becoming pregnant. Whatever it was, she tried hard not to show it. I'd hope that I could break through her barrier and have a night full of bliss. Even though she was afraid I knew she was willing because I'd captured her heart.

Again we settled into the bed kissing passionately. I caressed her breasts while lightly stroking her clitoris. I could taste the passion of her perspiration as her body heat was now at its boiling point. Pushing my finger deep inside her I was reminded by her tightness that she had never been to that point before, she was a virgin. As I was removing the last of her garments I could hear sounds from the other room as if Mo was begging and pleading for the pussy, but my focus was on my woman as I had her to the point of no return. As I spread her legs for entry that frightened look was once again prevalent.

"Are you sure you want to do this?" I asked.

"Yes, I'm sure," she responded.

Suddenly, Mo's girl shouted out, "It's Saturday and I told you I can't have sex tonight because I'm a Jehovah Witness!"

I tell you, Gem and I lost all passion as we went into hysteria. We laughed until we had nothing left. Mo got upset and started crying when he heard us laughing at him. He wanted to leave. I told him he must be fucking crazy if he thought I was going to leave because he didn't get any pussy.

"Rather than getting angry just wait until Sunday morning to tap that ass," I suggested.

The girl then decided she was not sleeping in the bed with Mo because he wouldn't stop crying. I knew I was not letting her chunky ass sleep with me so I told Gem to take her no-pussy-giving Jehovah-ass home. Realizing that a crying, limp dick had blown my chance of nailing the second finest bitch I had ever seen made me very angry.

Remaining cool I asked, "Are you okay, Mo?"

"Yeah, I'm all right."

"Good, now take your crying ass to sleep because I ain't going to give you no pussy either and I ain't no Jehovah Witness," I responded then fell out laughing again; and yes, he started crying in anger.

After being so close to Gem's hot, naked body I thirst for the day when I could hang my pole all up in her ass. I was like a white man's bloodhound on the trail of a nigger who had just escaped from the penitentiary. Her scent was upon me. My every thought was of being inside her, deep between her legs. I couldn't sleep at night from the constant chattering between my stiff dick and rock-hard nuts. I tried choking it but the tightness around the head made it worse; it felt like a tight pussy was upon it. I tried cold showers and hot showers but nothing would quench the thirst; I was having a penis uprise.

It was Friday night and I planned to work in her tight pussy all night long. My baby had come home with me after class and we prepared dinner together. Eating by candlelight I could see the sparkles of joy in her eyes; also, the happiness reflected from her high-yellow face revealed to me that she was in heat. I'd waited far beyond my kill time.

Romance before the big dance reverberated in my mind. I wanted to take her up past the high of a few days ago. I wanted to cream her before I whipped the milk. We kissed with intense passion. As I stroked her cunt I licked and sucked softly on the nipples of her grapefruit-size breasts. The deep moans, simultaneous with the flowing, warm juices were my barometer.

Begging, she screamed, "Please give it to me now," as she squirmed to my every touch. "I can't take no more...I got to have it," she continued.

Moving between her legs I said, "You put it in when you want it in."

She wasted no time guiding it straight to her bull's eye. She jumped as if to back away as I penetrated, but I grabbed that ass and held her steady while I worked the head little by little. She was wet, but still tight. Working it slowly, I kissed her vigorously, moving deeper inside her with every stroke. Her eyes began to roll back into her forehead, her body shivered with the swelling of my penis head; she was ready to explode. A deep caterpillar move made her scream, "Oh, my God...oh, shit!" at the loss of her virginity. The pain from a new beginning filled her space. Tears of joy danced down her cheeks as she came with delight.

"Did it hurt?" I asked in a somewhat concerned voice.

"A little," she responded.

But I knew it was more than a little being her first time, not to mention my size. Still inside her moving rhythmically I'd swollen beyond capacity.

"Work me, Baby...I want to feel that ass working," I said in utmost pleasure.

"I'm trying, Baby, I'm trying." Using her every ounce of energy she twirled her ass in an up-and-down motion.

"Oh, Baby...milk this dick," I said, as I shot off like a milked cow.

Upon the realization that I'd cum in her she went into deep depression; completely in a state of inertia. She remained that way for the rest of the night. The days that followed were not much better. I worried about her but didn't know what to do. That was a first for me, I was scared.

Sunday afternoon when I took her to her dorm she was still out of it so I decided to stay away until she came around. Later it was brought to my attention that Chinadoll's friend had dropped the 411 on me, revealing to Gem that Ny'lora was back home pregnant with my child; further, that we were to be married upon graduation. That was the same little witch who had concocted a bunch of lies causing Chinadoll to doubt me. Now she was doing the same thing to Gem and now it all made sense why Gem was so fearful about making love.

A few days later I cornered Miss Celie and demanded from her the reason why she was all up in my motherfucking business. Her response shocked the hell out of me.

"I've been desiring you since high school. Give me a chance and I'll be at your beck and call."

"Not a fucking chance. Now stay the fuck out of my business or I'll bash your ugly face in," I said, putting my hand in the form of a fist up in her face.

Gem and I stayed separated until we bumped into each other at the campus ballroom dance. She was looking irresistibly good. Reluctantly I asked if we could go somewhere and talk. She agreed. I drove to an isolated spot where I could spill my guts uninterrupted. On that night I was not too proud to beg.

I told her it was true that Ny'lora was pregnant with my baby but the part about us getting married after graduation was an outright lie.

"There has never been any discussion between Ny'lora and me about marriage, period!" I said.

I explained that I wasn't trying to deceive her, I had been waiting for the right time, and that time being the point where I felt in my heart that she was extra special to me and that point was right here, right now!

"I love you," I said.

She cried, saying how much she loved me and how badly she wanted us to be together. "I don't care about the other woman and the baby just as long as you tell me that I'm yours," she said.

Kissing the tears from her cheeks I hugged her tightly and spoke words of assurance, "Not only are you mine...I will forever be yours."

Rhapsody was upon her as she sang *I love you....I love you*, in medley.

Insisting that we had been apart much too long, she refused to go to her dormitory; instead, she wanted to go home with me. When we arrived at my crib Jet and his tall, dark, good-looking mate were in my bed whooping it up. Jet was my right hand man so that was okay. I preferred it that way. My instincts were telling me not to rush things so I put on some music and kept things simple. Around 12:30 a.m. Jet exited the room, rushing to get his lady home as she still lived with her mom.

I was sleepy but scared to death of asking Gem back in the room. After what had happened the last time I didn't know if Gem would freak out, go crazy, or kill me in my sleep. Being in tune with me she sensed that I was reluctant to ask her to bed.

"I'm alright," she said. "We can go to bed if you like."

As we got ready for bed I prayed that my dick was also tired.

Morning came quickly. After breakfast we spent the whole day together driving around and acting silly. Everyone wanted me to have my usual Saturday night party but I decided to spend the evening alone with Gem. After a long, muggy day Gem and I took a shower. We took our time, taking turns as we bathed each other, exploring and touching each and every sensitive spot. I was drawn to her body like metal to a magnet and I knew there was no way I could pass on that ass.

Everything was clean so I started tasting the honey of my bee. I didn't know what the hell was going to happen or who she would turn into, but I did know that I was going to fuck her to death. Blind, cripple, or crazy I was going to spank that ass. I picked her up and carried her from the shower straight to the bed, water dripping from both our bodies. As I licked her ass dry the heat was turned up. I worked that dick easy until I was able to bury it all the way to my nuts. I stroked her a long while as she came again and again.

She made love to me as good as anyone had. When she felt the head of my dick starting to swell she knew from before exactly what to do. I came with vengeance. Inundated in perspiration I got up to get a towel from the linen closet. Upon my return she was hysterical; her eyes were rolled back into her head as she cried. There was a demon in her and she was possessed in my bed, I thought. I felt scared. I was out of my element, I needed an exorcist. I kept waiting for her head to start spinning around.

All night long I watched her with no change to her condition. Around 8 a.m. I washed her body as she lay solemn and naked in the bed. With little help from her I dressed her then drove to the campus, put her out in front of the dorm, and watched as she walked up the stairs to her hall. I knew no matter how much I cared about her I could not endure her being traumatized each time we made love.

In my heart I knew she would remain in her own sacred space. Our brief beginning had come to an abrupt ending.

CHAPTER 23

GRADUATION PRESENTS

Graduation was about two months away, June 4, 1972. Ironically, Ny'lora was expecting to have my baby around the same time. She wanted to come to the graduation ceremony but her mother and I agreed that it would be too risky. Ny'lora was very audacious and insisted that she would be there if the baby didn't come. But I said no, and told her I didn't want to hear all that other lip jacking.

I found myself thinking of Gem quite often. I missed her terribly. Somehow, beyond my clouded judgment I knew that it was for the best this way; especially given my responsibility to Ny'lora and the baby. I'd been taught to be responsible for my actions good or bad. I saw the birth of my child as a good thing and was determined to meet my obligations head on.

I decided to give one last party that weekend in an attempt to pull out of my slight depression over losing Gem. My stereo system needed some work so I took it to the shop for an overhaul. A couple of buddies went along for the ride; we were just hanging out that Wednesday afternoon. While I was talking to the repairman in the back of the store one of the guys stole an expensive amplifier. That of course was without my knowledge. Stealing definitely was not a part of my character.

Upon returning to campus I was informed of the occurrence. Being on probation I immediately put them out of my car. The last thing I needed was to have police trouble at graduation time.

Later that evening I returned home to find six sheriff cars surrounding my trailer. I just kept on riding past my place and parked in back of Mavel's trailer, which was across from mine. When I entered through her rear door she started to interrogate me, "What have you done now? Why are you always in trouble?"

"I haven't done anything," I replied. "It wasn't me, someone else stole the amplifier."

I watched from her window as the sheriffs looked through my windows and underneath the trailer. About an hour later they left. Mavel gave me a card that the detective had left, asking me to call him. There was no way I was going to stay in that house that night so I begged Mavel to allow me to sleep at her crib, even if it was on the couch. At least I knew I could sleep good without fear of being highjacked in the middle of the night by the police.

I observed several sheriff cars passing by during the night, possibly looking for my car to be parked in front of the trailer. Early the next morning I slipped into the house, took a shower and got dressed then proceeded to the detective's office where I answered all of his questions correctly, except one.

"Do you know what happened to the amplifier?" he asked.

"No, sir. I was in the back with the technician and saw no one take anything," I replied. "However, there were two white people in the store when I came in," I continued. The look on his face told me that he had no defense against the shit I'd just put on him. He knew that I had two blacks with me but the owner of the store hadn't told him about the two white folks.

The water was now muddy. "You may go," was all that he could say.

The party went on as planned. I was not surprised when Gem didn't show up. In a way I was hoping that she would, even though I knew it was for the best if she didn't.

The party was really jumping and the spiked wine was doing its thing. About 10 p.m. the door opened and in strutted a brick house as if she owned the place. She was fine as old wine and knew it.

Afer requesting the DJ to play a slow jam, without hesitation, I encroached on her space.

"Would you like to dance?" I asked.

"Sure," she replied.

My boy, the DJ, was right on time when he played *Your Precious Love* by Jerry Butler—long with strong lyrics. To my surprise she knew who I was even though I didn't have a clue about her. She told me her name was Darlene. For the next hour we danced nonstop exclusively with each other. She had sent my depression packing.

About 11:30 p.m. the door opened again. It was Gem, looking good enough to eat. Immediately she spotted me on the dance floor with Darlene tightly clutched in my arms. I could see Gem starting to make her way through the crowd in my direction.

"Oh, shit!" I said.

"Is there a problem?" Darlene asked.

"Not really...just a friend I didn't expect to see anymore."

"I heard you two had broken up," she said. "Go ahead and take care of your business... I'll be around."

Finally reaching the spot where we were slow dancing Gem said to Darlene, "Do you mind if I dance with my man?"

"I ceased being your man a few weeks ago," I responded.

"I don't mind if you dance...I just don't know about him being your man," Darlene replied.

Cutting in, Gem put her arms around me and the fever started all over again. She was like that Almond Joy candy that was irresistibly good. Gem's seductive ways and good looks made her almost impossible to resist. Darlene was on the outside trying to get in and Gem was on the inside with me trying to get out.

I wanted to talk to Darlene so I could set up something for a later date but Gem interfered each time I attempted to move in her direction. Jet knew what was going on so he handled the situation with Darlene for me; he put her on the instant layaway plan, which meant, *Baby, hold on it won't be long because the heat is on.*

Even though I wanted Gem badly, I knew I had to terminate our relationship. She refused to leave that night, fearing that I would end up in the arms of the other woman. While I was giving my exodus speech she got naked and stretched out in my bed. For the first time in my life I didn't listen to my dick, which was panting at the mouth. My mind had overridden my dick's call to glory when it could not erase the memory of a night of horror.

Acting as if nothing I said mattered, she listened until she fell asleep. Being careful not to wake the dead I got up, made a pot of coffee and watched TV. When I took Gem back to her dorm the next morning I made it crystal clear that we had no future.

It was the weekend before graduation so I decided to visit Ny'lora and take the majority of my belongings home. I arrived to find my sugar in full bloom, looking like she should have had the baby a month ago. The due date was the first week of June.

We were expecting her to go into labor any day. All she talked about was going to my graduation. Nothing seemed more important than seeing me march across the stage. As eager as she was I felt it was too dangerous for her to make the four-hour trip so I put my foot down and gave her a flat out no.

"I'll see you at the graduation!" was her response.

***

I'd met all of my requirements including passing the final semester. I'd been exempt from taking final exams since all my grades averaged B or better. I was just hanging loose waiting for the big day.

On Thursday, two days before graduation, I ran into Darlene on the set. "Did you get your business straightened out with Gem?" she asked.

"I did and thanks for being so understanding," I said.

"I guess I won't see you anymore after you graduate?" she queried.

"Who knows what the future will bring."

"Just in case the cards don't have me as part of your future I would like to give you a graduation present tomorrow, and I insist," she said.

"Well, all of my family is coming in tomorrow at 6 p.m. so I won't have any time."

"No problem," she said, "I'll meet you at noon and enjoy you until 5 p.m, if that's okay with you?" she said with a smile.

"Baby, I can't think of anything I'd rather do than spend the afternoon with you...with your fine self," I said. "I have rooms reserved at the Rhodeway Inn on Appallachee Parkway...meet me there at noon on the dot."

Darlene showed up fifteen minutes early. After checking in I left all the keys, except the one I had, at the front desk; that way I wouldn't have to be on the lookout for my family. Anyway, I figured I'd take a snooze after I got finished with Miss Darlene.

We didn't want to waste any time so we headed straight for the room, which was on the third floor. Once in the room I immediately undressed myself. What took place wasn't about romance but about giving a performance that would leave a lifetime impression.

I leaned down to kiss her as she sat on the edge of the bed. While undoing her blouse I caressed and sucked her nipples. Laying her on the bed I removed what was left of her clothes as she raised her hips to help me. With four hours of time I wanted her on top first. I wanted to tap into her energy source before tapping into my own. She worked that pussy good while taking every inch of my dick. I raised her shoulders straight up to allow my cock to rub across her clitoris with every stroke. I sent her ass into a frenzy as she came with the force of a waterfall. Cum ran down my penis filling up my belly button while soaking the bed beneath us. I put her on her knees at the edge of the bed and stood up behind her. I got that pussy working like a fine tuned machine.

"Oh, God, this is too much... I can't take all this dick," she shouted.

"You can take it, Baby, just keep that pussy pumping," I said.

I hit a deep spot. She jumped forward and said, "No more...no more!"

Laying her on her back I raised her legs above her head. Lifting my body I inserted myself deep inside her, so deep I heard a grunt, followed by a fart from her ass on the up stroke. Ramming dick, she screamed, begging me to hurt her some more.

"Oh, God! Nobody can fuck me like you do," she said.

"Do you like this dick?"

"Yes, Baby, I love this dick."

"Who's pussy is this?"

"It's your pussy. I'm your bitch!"

Suddenly, without warning, the door swung wide open.

"Surprise!" they yelled to the crack of my ass.

"Oh, shit!" I shouted.

About the Author

Johnny Archer was born in St. Petersburg, Florida – the youngest of six children in a family of four girls and two boys. He grew up in the projects of Jordan Park, which he credits for his will to survive. He attended Florida Agricultural & Mechanical University (FAMU), where he received a B.S. degree in Mathematics.

After 14 years working within the aerospace industry, he decided he had had enough of the bureaucracy that at times was less than fair for black engineers.

Today, Mr. Archer owns a successful construction company based in South Florida. His company specializes in residential and commercial construction.

This is the author's first novel and one that he is very proud of since writing was his worse subject.

Additional copies may be ordered on-line from

Writers and Poets.com, LLC

www.writersandpoets.com

sales@writersandpoets.com

Special discounts are available for libraries and organizations

---

Other books published by Writers and poets.com, LLC

Threesome: Where Seduction, Power and Basketball Collide

by Brenda L. Thomas

Memoir: Delaware County Prison

By Reginald L. Hall